THE WAITRESS

EMILY SHINER

INKUBATOR
BOOKS

Published by Inkubator Books
www.inkubatorbooks.com

ISBN (eBook): 978-1-83756-281-7
ISBN (Paperback): 978-1-83756-282-4
ISBN (Hardback): 978-1-83756-283-1

PROLOGUE

Darkness pressed in on both sides of the road, the rays of the full moon only breaking through the branches from time to time. The car zipped along the road, headlights piercing the dark, sending nocturnal creatures scattering away from the roar of the engine and deeper into the woods.

There was someone up ahead. Someone walking, using a cane, their back bent and crooked, one hand resting on their lower back as if that would be enough to stop whatever pain dwelled there. Headlights caught the figure, and they turned, adjusting their grip on the cane.

The steering wheel jerked to the right. Hard.

Foot pressed down on the gas.

Rocks from the gravel road spit up into the undercarriage of the vehicle, scattering out to the sides, leaving clouds of dust in their wake.

There was more than enough time to brake. More than enough time to stop the car, to jerk the wheel back, to slide down into the ditch, and hit a tree.

And not hit a person.

The pedestrian couldn't move. Frozen like a deer, they stared into the headlights, then moved away, doing their best to get out of the car's path, but each step was too slow. Their foot slipped in the gravel. They listened for brakes, a squealing, something that would let them know this was just a bad dream, but that wasn't what reached their ears. They heard the sound of gravel spitting, an engine revving.

Someone laughing?

The car slammed into the pedestrian, meat crunching against metal; then the driver braked, sending the person flying. They landed in a ditch, their body crumpled. Their cane rolled once, bounced, then lay still.

The car reversed. The engine growled. Slowly the driver angled the car down the gravel road and pressed down on the gas, taking their time now.

From somewhere through the trees, a person watched.

1

TUESDAY

My old Camry is held together with prayers and duct tape, but it somehow rumbles down the road to my house, spitting up gravel behind me as I carefully navigate around the potholes that are forming in the road. Even with only a handful of neighbors on the street, the road continues to deteriorate, but it's not a state road, so guess who doesn't care?

The state.

My chest feels tight as I nose onto my driveway. Parking the car by the sagging outbuilding, I step out onto brushy patches of grass and hurry to the house. Dave should have been on the bus home today. He should already be here. But the fact he didn't text me to let me know he got home, that nothing was wrong...

Well, it concerns me.

The front porch is a little saggy, but I ignore how the boards need to be ripped up and replaced as I shove my key in the front lock. Being a single mom is hard no matter where you live and what job you have. But being a single mom when the best you can do is working at the diner in town?

It's tricky to make ends meet. I'm much more worried about getting food on the table and not nearly as concerned about whether or not the boards on the porch need to be replaced.

"Dave, I'm home." When I call out for my son, I slap a smile on my face. That's the only way to mask the frustration running through me right now.

"In the kitchen," he calls back, his voice low—lower than it was yesterday, I swear, he just keeps growing—and I drop my purse, hurrying to him.

"How was your day?" I'm nervous, standing in the doorway. It's silly, isn't it? To be so nervous when faced with your own child? I carried him, grew him, kissed his little head, and fed him. It's always been the two of us against the world, and I love Dave more than I love anything or anyone else.

But I'm still nervous.

He stands, unfolding himself from the chair at the table, then crosses his arms as he looks at me. "The school wants to talk to you."

My heart sinks. *Of course they do.* One look at the expression on Dave's face and I already know things must be bad.

"Dave," I begin, but he waves his hand at me. It's now that I realize, with a start, I have to look up at my son. He towers over me, a smirk on his face, and until this moment he's never looked more like his father.

"Mom, chill. It's just school. Just stuff like math, even. When am I ever going to use math?" He shrugs. "I thought you'd want to know. I stayed here until you got off work just so I could tell you to your face."

"I can't keep taking time off work to handle whatever you

have going on at school. I've told you that, Dave. Do you want me to lose my job, because that's what's going to happen next. Richard told me—"

"Richard needs to get over himself. He wears his little ties so tight it's a wonder he can even breathe." Dave mimes choking himself with a tie. "Come on, you hate the diner anyway. So what if you get fired?"

I take a deep breath. "I can't get fired because then I'd have to find another job. It's not easy to do that, Dave, not when I want to work the same hours that you're in school so I can be home when you're home in the evenings and most weekends."

And so I can make sure you don't get into any more trouble.

"Then get an office job, Mom. I don't know. But you need to talk to the principal." He grabs a sheet of paper from the table and thrusts it into my hands. "Here's the information. Call her."

"Call her, right," I mutter, scanning the paper for information on what my son did this time.

Skipping school? Been there, done that.

Smoking behind the auditorium? I don't have any idea where he got the cigarettes, but it's impossible to argue with a teacher who said they saw him out there.

Punching a kid? There's really no defense for that one. Maybe if Dave were some scrawny kid, maybe if he were in theater and wore Coke-bottle glasses and he was just standing up for himself against the school bully. But he's huge, the football coach falling all over himself in an effort to get him on the team. However, there's a rule against your players getting suspended all the time.

And that's the one way Dave is reliable. Suspensions.

But this one is new. He intimidated a new teacher. The science teacher, apparently.

"Tell me about the science teacher," I say, reaching out and grabbing Dave's arm before he can sneak past me and out of the room. "It says you intimidated him."

"It wasn't hard." Dave grins, flexing.

I feel his muscles shift under my grip, but I don't let go. "Why can't you just be nice? Why do you have to be—"

"So much like my father?" He finishes the question for me, but there's no anger in his voice. For the first time since this conversation began, he just looks tired. Beat up.

Like a little kid looking for validation and love.

"You're better than him," I whisper. "I told you I'd always keep you safe from him, that I'd always make sure nothing bad ever happened to you. Don't be like him, Dave."

The innocent look is still there. He still looks like my baby, like the toddler who would cling to my legs when I had to go to work. I see him in all of the stages of childhood I loved and lost and would fight to get back because I love him that much. That's the thing about mothers and our children —we don't just see the current version of our child standing in front of us when we look at our kids.

We see every stage of their life, all the times they came to us looking for help, all the times they needed us and we were there. This stage with Dave is the most difficult, by far, but that doesn't mean we can't get through it.

"I'll call in to take some time off tomorrow to talk to your principal," I finally say with a sigh. "But I need you to meet me halfway. You're a good kid, okay? You don't need to act like your father."

He's silent for a moment. *Maybe I got through to him.*

"Just take care of it for me, would you? I don't have time

to deal with this. I can't help it if the science teacher is a dweeb." He shrugs his shoulder, and I let go of him, stepping back as he leaves the kitchen.

The stairs groan under his weight, and I close my eyes, listening to his footsteps as he makes his way down the hall to his room. This house is falling apart around us, but there isn't anywhere else I can go.

My cell phone is heavy in my hand as I dial Richard. I already know what he's going to say.

Get your stuff together, Anne Marie.

It's not my fault your son is out of control.

Either make him get his act together or find somewhere else to work. You can't keep calling out like this.

There is nowhere else. And Dave needs me. He's difficult, yes. Trouble. He gets on my last nerve and pushes my buttons. I wouldn't admit it to anyone, but sometimes my son even scares me.

But I'll do anything for him.

2

WEDNESDAY

The halls of Skyridge High are packed with students, most of them taller than me, all of them loud, in a hurry, pushing their way to their next class. I angle myself out of the crush of bodies and pause by the cement brick wall, pressing my hands flat against it as I wait out the crowd. I was supposed to be here for my meeting with the principal twenty minutes ago, but it was busy at the diner, and I hated leaving Carla there to fend for herself.

The bell rings, a loud toll, and the halls magically clear out. As soon as I'm alone with just a few stragglers, I turn toward the office, hurrying now as I do my best to avoid being much later than I already am.

"I'm here to see Principal Byler," I say to the receptionist up front. Her long blonde hair is piled on the top of her head, and she looks over blue cat-eye glasses at me. "I have an appointment," I add.

She sniffs. Clicks her mouse. Looks back at me. "Mrs.

Byler has numerous appointments throughout the day. Looks like you were late for yours."

"I know." I gesture to my apron in apology. I'd wanted to take it off before coming here, but I hadn't had time. "I'm sorry, work was crazy, and I couldn't get away. I hurried over here as soon as possible. Believe me, I know how important this is."

A sigh. She gives her head a little shake like she's trying to convince herself to help me, then juts her thumb over her shoulder at a half-open door. "She's in there. Waiting."

"Thank you," I say, already hurrying around her desk to the open door. Behind me I hear as she calls the principal on an office phone to let her know I'm coming. I step through into the principal's office and close the door behind me. As many times as I've been in here, I still feel like a little kid who's in trouble. I'm an adult, but when it comes to Dave and keeping him out of trouble, all bets are off.

"Ms. Kerns," Principal Byler says, "please sit."

I do, eyeballing the woman who sits across from me at the huge oak desk in her office, her perfectly manicured fingers steepled together in front of her face. Her makeup is flawless; her hair looks like something off a runway. In contrast I feel like a sack of potatoes.

"Thank you so much for coming in," she says, then unsteeples her fingers and leans forward a bit like she's trying to drink me in. "I wanted to talk to you about Dave."

"Of course," I say, because what other response is there? *Oh, I thought you called me here to tell you about the specials of the day?*

"As you know, when we spoke last week, I was very worried about his behavior." She holds up a hand like I'm going to protest, as if I'm not sitting right here listening to her, waiting for her to tell me how sad she'd be about having to kick him out of school and send him to the alternative high school. "But things have changed. He's not just smoking cigarettes during recess."

"He told me about the science teacher," I offer, wanting to get this over with as quickly as possible. "I know there was an incident with him. Dave has expressed remorse over how he handled things."

"He did?" Her eyebrows, perfectly manicured, crash together. "That's different, because when I spoke to him, he told me his teacher *had it coming*." She lets that one soak in for a minute before continuing, "I don't want to threaten you. That's not my style. But you and I both know this isn't a tenable situation. Some kids just aren't compatible with regular school."

"And you think Dave might be one of those kids?" I'm perched on the edge of the chair, unwilling to sit back and get comfortable. "Are you telling me you're going to kick him out?"

"I'm telling you that I have every right to." Her voice drops a bit. "I don't want to do that to you. I know you're working hard, doing your best. But sometimes our best isn't enough. I don't want to punish you, but maybe my school isn't the right fit for your son. Maybe we need to help him. Get him in somewhere else. What do you think?"

I think I feel the beginning of a headache coming on, and I close my eyes, trying to gather my thoughts. "Dave is a good kid," I begin, but she cuts me off.

"Ms. Kerns, I don't want to sit here and insult you, nor do I want you to sit here and talk to me like I haven't been dealing with your son's shenanigans all year long. He's been in trouble over and over. Smoking," she says, holding up a finger. "Drinking." She adds another finger. "Fighting and cheating on tests." There go two more. "Now he's gone so far as to threaten a teacher. At what point would you have me say that enough is enough?"

"Please." My voice shakes, and I swallow hard to try again. "Mrs. Byler, I know you don't know me very well, and you certainly don't have the best opinion of me or my son, but I promise you, I'm working on it."

"How?" She leans back, crosses her arms. "How are you working on it? What steps, exactly, are you taking to ensure that these problems with Dave are addressed? I want assurance that they're in the past, but I don't know if you can honestly give me that."

I roll my head from side to side. There's the start of a tension headache, little pinpricks of pain that will burst into an overwhelming crush all around my skull if this conversation doesn't wrap up immediately.

"You have to trust me," I say, but she shakes her head, putting her hand down on the desk between us. It isn't loud. She doesn't slam it down, doesn't even make a sound, but it's firm enough that I know when I'm being cut off.

"I've already started the paperwork to have him transferred to a remedial school."

Is that pity in her voice? The thought of her pitying me being a single mom trying as hard as I can but still somehow always failing, of not knowing what to do because Dave is out of control, is sickening.

"Don't sign the paperwork," I beg, leaning forward. "Dave's trying, he really is. If you transfer him, then he'll know that you don't believe in him. That nobody believes in him. I promise you I'm working on it. I'm doing everything I can to help him."

"Counseling?"

I shake my head.

"Medication?"

"What? No." I frown at her. "I'm mothering him. Taking care of him. His father...well, Dave doesn't know him, and for good reason. He wasn't kind. Wasn't a gentle man." My fingers circle my wrist without me realizing what I'm doing. How many times did he grab me right there, leaving bruises behind?

"You can't blame a father for how his son turned out."

"Do you have children?"

Her eyes narrow. "Biological ones? No. But I have hundreds of children here, and I have to keep them safe from students like Dave."

"One last chance." I breathe the words like a prayer. How many hours have I spent on my knees while Dave was out and about, praying that he'd come to his senses, stop acting out, be a better son?

Too many.

The principal sighs. She rolls her eyes and reaches for her coffee cup, taking a long sip before she puts it back down and finally speaks. "One more chance. But I promise you, after that, he's gone. Done. Don't pass go; don't collect two hundred dollars. Understand?"

"Thank you. What you're doing for Dave, I can't tell you enough how much I appreciate it." I pause, wondering how thick I dare to lay it on. A bit more. "It takes a village, you know."

"It sure does. And sometimes the village has to work harder than other times." She laughs, resting her fingers against her throat like she's fully expecting a photographer to jump out and shoot her for an ad campaign.

Bitches R Us, or something.

"I agree. Thank you." I want to tell her more, tell her how hard I try, how much work it is to be a single mother, but I see the slim wedding band on her finger right next to the huge diamond. Women like her don't get it. They don't know what it's like to be willing to bleed yourself dry to ensure your child will be taken care of, will be safe, will be loved.

They don't know how far a mother is willing to go.

3

"Well, I kept my job," I say, taking a bite of Hamburger Helper before looking up at my son. He's sitting across from me, one elbow on the table, shoveling food into his mouth like he's afraid I'm going to take his plate away from him. "But Richard made it very clear that if I call out again without someone *having died*—his words, not mine—that I shouldn't expect him to be so kind in the future."

Dave shrugs. Scrapes the last bite of food into a pile, then uses his thumb to shove it onto his fork. "Good for you, Mom. You can keep going to the diner, wearing that stupid apron, and simpering so people give you tips. Do you want me to applaud you?"

"A 'thank you' would be nice," I say, putting my fork down to look at him. "And use your knife. Why else do you think we have them?"

"Too late. Maybe tomorrow." He shoves back from the table and stretches. "I need the car keys. I'm going out."

"Out?" I chuckle. "It's a school night. Where in the world

do you need to be going right now? It's going to get dark in a few hours, and you know you're not allowed to drive at night on your provisional license."

He smiles at me, showing me all his teeth. "Would you feel better if I promise to be home by dark?"

My stomach sinks. Getting Dave his driver's license had seemed like a good idea at the time. I'd thought that a little responsibility would be good for him, that he might be more helpful around the house. I had visions of him running to the store to pick things up for me, swinging by the bank, that sort of thing.

But none of that has happened. The only time he wants to use the car is when he has something to do. I think he's gone to the store for me once, and that was when I had the flu and there wasn't anything in the house for either of us to eat. I'd asked for crackers and some bread to make dry toast, and he came back with a steak for himself.

"Give me the keys, Mom." His voice is stronger. Lower. I feel the way it curls around my neck like a noose, and I nod, pulling my keys from my pocket before I know what I'm doing.

"Just be safe," I say. "And tell me, where are you going?"

"Don't worry about it. I'll be home later." He swipes the keys from the table and dangles them from his finger. "See you later, Mom."

And then he's gone. The front door slams shut, and I sink down lower in my chair. A moment later, the Camry roars to life, and Dave seesaws it back and forth in the driveway to turn all the way around before gunning it. I can't see the road we live on from our house, but I can hear the way gravel flies out behind the tires as he drives away.

For a moment, I close my eyes. The road isn't straight.

There are curves you have to be careful around, curves that drop down to almost one lane. It's a terrible place to live, but it was the best I could do at the time. Whenever Dave drives off like this, I have an awful mental image of him missing a curve, flying into a tree, metal and skin wrapped around bark.

But no crash comes, and I shake my head, clearing the vision. My appetite gone, I clean up the table, putting the leftovers in the fridge. On second thought, I rearrange the shelves, pushing the leftovers to the back.

If he sees them right up front when he gets home, then it's very likely he'll pull them out and eat them, but we'll need them tomorrow. I do feel a little guilty hiding food from my son like this, but it's not like he'd listen to me if I just asked him not to eat it.

As a little kid, sure. Dave would have listened to me. Younger Dave would have done whatever I asked him to, and done it with a smile on his face.

That Dave may be gone for now, but I'll do anything to get him back.

It's thoughts like that that keep me from giving up.

Just as I'm about to start washing dishes, my phone pings. A silly grin spreads across my face when I see who the text is from. Not Richard, thank goodness. Not another threat from Mrs. Byler.

Benji.

> Just got some gas. Thinking about you. I hope Dave isn't being too much of a handful.

After reading the text out loud, I sigh and close my eyes

for a minute. With everything going on with Dave, I sometimes forget that I have Benji on my side.

Of course, I wish he were home more. I wish I got to see him during the week. And I wish Dave were kinder to him. He never loved the idea of me dating anyone, but Benji is such a great guy. I don't know why Dave can't seem to get along with him.

My fingers fly as I tap out my response.

Just missing you. Dave is...Dave. See you this weekend?

I press send.

I'll try.

His response is immediate and not what I wanted to hear from him. I frown.

I miss him and want to talk to him. I want to have his arms around me so the stress of my life can melt away. But as much as I wish I could talk to him about Dave and get his opinion on what's going on, he's not interested in hearing about it. He knows Dave is a handful, and he knows Dave doesn't like him. I don't like having to keep the two of them separate, but I don't have a choice, not if I want to keep Benji in my life.

And I do. My life is difficult, but Benji is one of the best things in it. I want him. And Dave. That's all.

But if someone forced me to choose? If someone held a gun to my head and made me pick Benji or Dave?

Easy. I'd pick my son. No question.

4

SATURDAY

Two days pass without incident, and I've somehow lucked out into having Saturday off. It's a bit of a trade-off, of course, like most things in life. Not working Saturday means I can spend the morning lounging around the house, drinking coffee, and reading. I can soak up the sun that makes its way through the windows or even sit outside on the back patio if the weather is nice. I can feel like a normal person with a normal job and a normal life, and I don't have to come home limping because I was on my feet for so many hours.

The trade-off is that I won't make any money this morning. I won't walk away with my pockets full of tips from the Saturday breakfast crowd, and I won't be able to sneak something from the bakery case when Richard isn't looking.

Still, I push those thoughts from my mind. Best to focus on the positive right now, which is that I get to enjoy my day. And I don't think Dave has any plans, which means I get to spend it with him, too. I top off my coffee and consider pouring him a cup, but even though it's already a bit past eight, he's not up.

He stumbled in yesterday after I was already in bed. I considered checking on him to see if he needed anything, but I was too tired to move. He'll need coffee, I'm sure, but I'll leave it in the pot for him.

Taking my cup, I walk out the back door, making sure to shut the screen door behind me. It's still early spring, but the mosquitos in the South tend to be big enough to carry off a house cat, and I'm not messing with them. I might get bit out here, but I can slap them away, but dealing with the bloodsuckers on my face while I'm sleeping?

The thought makes me shiver as I drop into a chair.

Just as I'm enjoying the silence, my phone chirps at me. Just the possibility of having to go into work this morning causes my stomach to drop and makes me sit up straight. Surely not. Surely Richard wouldn't call me in on my day off, not when I'm so excited about not going to work.

Slowly, like it's a snake that might bite me, I pull my phone from my pocket. It's a brick compared to newer models and runs slow, but it works. I tap on the screen, waiting a moment for it to respond.

Did you see the news?

Carla. I sigh, then lean my head back, closing my eyes. As far as neighbors go, she could be worse. I guess. If your comparison was Jeffrey Dahmer. Carla is busty and loves to flirt, which is why she makes so much money at the diner, but she's a terrible neighbor.

The self-appointed mayor of our crappy little road, I swear she sits at her front window with binoculars pressed to her face every hour that she's not working. When Dave got his driver's license, she offered to drive me to work when we shared shifts, but I couldn't do it.

She's just...a lot. She's a lot.

Haven't turned on the TV.

I send the text, then pause. Do I engage? Do I ask her what possibly could have happened that she'd be texting me right now? I probably should, but before I get the chance, my phone buzzes and lights up.

Old Mr. George died last night.

"Oh, that's sad," I say, even though there isn't anyone around to hear me. Mr. George lives on our street and is a crotchety old man whom I don't interact with, but still...it's always sad when someone in your sphere of acquaintances dies. "Probably just gave up the ghost after Jan died so many years ago. We all knew it was going to happen."

I shrug. Put my phone down.

But why would that be on the news?

I grab my phone, about to ask Carla, when it buzzes again.

It was a hit-and-run. On our street.

"Oh my God." I drop the phone in my lap like it burned me and press my hand against my chest. That's what I've always been afraid of, living on this crappy little road. People go so fast, and it's difficult to see around the curves. With trees pressing right up against both sides of the road, it would be almost impossible to get out of the way.

My phone rings.

"Hi, Carla," I say, standing up, my coffee forgotten. "What in the world is going on?" Thick trees press in on all sides of my property. In the winter, when they drop their leaves, I can see flashes of color through them. The red of my neighbor's car, the bright yellow of a taxi.

But now, in late spring, the green is so thick, so alive, that it's impossible to see through it. I remarked once to Dave that someone could be standing five feet into the woods and I'd have no idea they were there.

I shiver.

"Mr. George was out walking last night. You know how he does, tottering along the side of the road like he hadn't a care in the world. And you know he's almost deaf?"

"I know," I say, because it's clear from the long pause she expects some sort of response.

"Well, this morning Taylor was going to work. You know Taylor, down the road? Drives that black Jeep?"

I don't know Taylor. I've never seen the person, nor their Jeep. Heck, I don't even know if Taylor is a man or a woman. "Sure do," I say.

"Well, she was driving into work and saw him on the side of the road. Thought he'd fallen, apparently, because he'd been hobbling around on his cane. Canes and a gravel road don't really mix, you know. She stopped to check on him, and he was dead. The police say he was hit."

I take a deep breath. Somewhere in the bushes, a little wren screams her fool head off at me, telling me to get away from her nest, but I can't move. "And you said it's on the news?"

"Sure is. You can turn on the TV and watch it with me."

"I'm fine," I say, swallowing hard. "Do they know who hit him?"

"Not yet." Her voice lowers a bit, gets muffled. I can easily imagine her cupping her hand around the phone to prevent anyone else from hearing what she's about to say. "Honestly, it's not much of a loss. He was a terrible man, you know."

"I had no idea."

"I saw him kick a cat one time. Just an old feral cat looking for something to eat. He kicked it when he thought nobody else was looking. People always show their true colors when they think they're alone."

"That's terrible, but he didn't deserve to die like this."

"Maybe not. Or maybe it's karma."

I can imagine how she's shrugging right now, like a broken marionette with one shoulder jerking up and down, over and over. Carla loves gossip. Thrives on it the way some people thrive on love and kindness. If she says Mr. George kicked a cat, then he probably did, but this was still a terrible way to die.

I'm thinking about my newly deceased neighbor and the last time I saw him—hunched over, staring at his mailbox—when I realize Carla is still talking.

"...police will probably be around to talk to you soon, Anne Marie. I just thought you'd want to know. I swear, I'm the only one on the street who knows anything that's going on. If it weren't for me, you still wouldn't have any clue. Anyway, I need to let everyone else know. See you at work Monday!"

Then she's gone, the silence in my ear so abrupt it's almost surprising. Turning off my screen, I slip my phone back into my pocket. The thought of drinking my coffee turns my stomach, and I dump out my mug, then head inside.

The peaceful morning I thought I was going to get to enjoy? Ruined. Part of me is envious of Dave, upstairs, still asleep. He's immune to anything going on in the world right now and will stay that way until he gets up.

I sigh and walk into the house. At the kitchen sink I run water into my mug and stare out the window at my Camry. It's pulled up closer to the house than I normally park it, but that's because Dave is such a careless driver. He's always in a hurry, always trying to get things done faster than they need to be.

He parked on the scrubby grass right in front of our porch. I frown, heat rushing to my cheeks. It's one thing for him to be rude to me, it's another for him to be disrespectful of the house and how hard I work to keep it looking nice. Grabbing my keys from the counter where he tossed them, I walk out to my car to back it up.

It's a beater, all I could afford when I needed a new car. There are more dents and dings in the front bumper than I could count, but it's still my car. I trace my fingers along the hood as I walk to the driver's door. Get in. Start the car.

Back it up.

On my way back into the house, I pause and turn to look at my car. So many dents.

My mind races.

No. It's not possible. It's not something I want to even consider.

Surely I'd know if there were another dent.

5

Dave stumbles downstairs while I have the news on in the living room. I've pulled the easy chair across the room to get as close as possible to the TV so I didn't wake him. Even though the sound is low, I'm so focused on what's being said that I don't realize my son is behind me until he puts his hand on my shoulder.

"Mom."

I jump, then scream, whipping around to look up at him. "Oh my God, Dave, you can't sneak up on me like that!" My heart hammers uselessly in my chest, a bird in a cage, and I take a deep breath to try to calm down. "Did you just get up?"

"Yep." He answers me, but his eyes are locked on the TV behind me. "What's going on?"

"Mr. George was hit yesterday." I fumble for the remote and click the volume button to turn it up, turning around to watch the TV as I do. "Carla called me this morning. Said he was hit on our road. Can you imagine?"

Dave doesn't respond. I hear the floor shift as he walks to grab a straight-back chair and drag it to sit next to me.

"That's terrible."

"It is." I don't look at my son; my eyes are glued to the screen. Even though I've been watching it for twenty minutes now, I haven't learned anything more than what Carla told me. The police have no idea who hit our neighbor. They don't know exactly when it happened. The shots of the thick woods and our gravel road are so nondescript that it could be anywhere in the county.

A moment later, however, the scene changes, and a street sign appears. *Grace Road.*

Dave catches his breath.

"That's us," I say, reaching out to touch his arm. "I knew Carla was telling the truth, because why would she lie, but still. It's weird to see, isn't it?"

Dave nods.

An officer appears on the screen. "We're asking anyone who has any information about what happened last night to George Reece to contact our tip line. Until the driver of the car is caught, we won't rest. We need to make sure we handle what happened, and that everyone else living on the street is safe."

I mute the TV. "It's just so sad," I say, feeling like I'm repeating myself. "I can't believe he's dead."

"I thought you didn't like him." Dave eyeballs me before collapsing on the sofa. The look he throws over his shoulder at the TV is casual; then he looks back at me.

"I didn't," I say, shrugging. "Well, I guess that's not fair because I didn't really know him. But to die like that? He had to be scared. It had to be awful."

Dave doesn't respond. He's quieter than I've seen him in

a while. Normally he has some kind of smart retort to anything I say, especially if there are emotions involved. He's never been one to want to share how he feels about anything though. When I've asked him what's on his mind in the past, he'd usually get frustrated with me.

"Anyway, that's enough of that," I say, turning off the TV. "Would you like breakfast?" I brace myself, fully expecting him to laugh at me for offering to make him food, or to tell me he can handle it on his own. Even though I know how he's going to respond, of course I'm still going to offer to make him something to eat. He's my son.

"That sounds great, thanks." Dave stands and walks into the kitchen, leaving me to stare at his back.

What just happened?

Confused, I follow him into the kitchen. What would be even stranger is if he were already at the stove, turning on a burner, getting butter melted in the pan for me to make him some eggs, but he's not. He pours himself a cup of coffee and sits down at the table, an expectant look on his face.

At least that's normal. "So what are your plans for the day?" I ask as I open the fridge and rummage around for cheese and eggs. He loves cheesy scrambled eggs with toast, and I busy myself getting everything ready while he answers.

"I was going to go out with friends, but I think I might take the day off."

I pause, the egg held above the bowl, ready for me to crack it. "Take the day off?"

"From going out."

"That's nice." My throat feels tight and my movements robotic as I crack and whisk the eggs. Swallowing hard, I decide to push it. "Do you think you could help me in the backyard? We lost some limbs in that big storm a week or so ago, and I need them cleaned up."

The eggs sizzle as I pour them into the hot pan. I stir them before sprinkling salt and pepper. I keep my back to Dave while I wait for him to answer because I don't want him to know how hopeful I am that he'll help me.

"I could do that, sure."

Now I swear something is going on. It feels like all the times I've hoped he'd be better, all the times I've said little prayers into the dark before bed, asking someone to turn him back into the sweet son I've always loved, have finally been answered. What I've wanted so badly has come true.

Yet it's almost too good to be true.

Moving faster now, I plate his meal and pour myself another cup of coffee before joining him at the table. Dave doesn't say anything while he eats, and I don't have much to say, either. This is strange. It feels new and exciting, but uncomfortable and fragile, like one wrong move could bring everything falling down around my head.

Sometimes Dave reminds me so much of his father that it scares me. I knew I could never raise a child with him, so when he walked out of our lives, I didn't fight it. I didn't go looking for him, and I certainly never fell to my knees begging him to come back.

I got us this terrible little house and a terrible little job and a terrible little Camry. I've done everything in my power to make sure Dave turns out as good as possible, more like me than his father. But it's always felt like an uphill climb, like I'm dragging myself through thick mud using only my fingernails. No matter how hard I've tried to make Dave be good, like me, he's like his father.

Partying. Drinking. Going out all hours of the night with

his friends. Taking my car without asking and bringing it back without gas. I wouldn't suffer abuse at the hands of his father, but I've sure put up with it from his son.

I don't even realize that I've chuckled until Dave says something. He has his fork halfway to his mouth and is staring at me.

"Did I miss a joke?"

I stiffen, ready for the animosity that's sure to follow, but no venom drips from his words. His eyebrows are soft and inquisitive, his expression gentle. He doesn't look like he'll get angry at my response.

I have to remind myself that he's only sixteen. Just a boy, not a man like his father.

"Nope, I'm just happy." I take a sip of my coffee and hold my mug out for him to tap his in cheers. To my surprise, he does. Even though I'm shocked, I do my best to hide it so he doesn't get frustrated with me.

"Well, that was delicious," he says, then rises from the table. I automatically reach for his plate, ready to take it to the sink to wash it, but he beats me to it. I notice that he doesn't wash it for me, but he does put it in the sink, which is more than he's done in the past.

"I'm so glad," I say. "Why don't you grab your boots? I'll get us some work gloves from the outbuilding, and we can tackle those branches before it gets hot out. It's going to be humid today and might rain later, so if we can take care of the yard before then, it will be better."

"Sounds good." He leaves the kitchen, heading upstairs, and I walk to the front door. The dishes can wait until later.

I wasn't joking about the day getting hot and humid. Best to handle everything outside now, before it gets so gross that it feels like you're swimming just walking across the yard. In the living room I slip on my old work boots, then grab the front door and throw it open.

The man standing on my front porch has his hand raised to knock. I gasp at the sight of him, and he takes a small step back before catching himself and straightening up as tall as he can stand. The badge on his chest seems to glow even in the dim light of the porch.

Police. On my porch. His jaw is tight, his eyes are dark. He squints, looking past me into the house, and I'm just grateful he can't read my mind, that he has no idea what I was thinking about Dave earlier, about what a mess he is, about how...bad he can be.

Because, right now, as good as Dave is, as much as I prayed he'd be better, I'm worried.

6

"Officer, hello." I wipe my hand on my pants, hoping he won't notice the motion and realize how nervous I am to be face-to-face with him. "What can I do for you?"

"I'm here to talk about your neighbor George Reece. He was hit while walking on the road last night and left to die." The officer cranes his neck to look past me. "Are you the only one home?"

Heavy footsteps hammer down the stairs behind me.

"My son, Dave, is here." I turn, gesturing for Dave to join me at the door. "But this morning was the first either of us heard about it. Our neighbor called to fill us in, and then we turned on the news. It's terrible."

"It is." The officer clears his throat.

His badge says Waddell on it. Everything about his uniform screams that he's completely in control. The lines of his pants are all sharp and crisp, like he ironed them into place. His name tag is perfectly level. Even his duty belt, which looks too heavy for anyone to wear comfortably on their hips, sits on him like it belongs there.

"This your car?" He gestures to my Camry, and I nod. "Looks like it's been through the wringer."

"It's all I could afford," I offer, hating that I feel like I have to defend myself and my mode of transportation. "But it's reliable."

"Pretty dented up." He's turning away from me now, moving quickly as he steps off the porch and into the scrubby grass to get a better look at the car. "Any new dents on there?"

I freeze. "No, none. Like I said, I bought what I could afford, and unfortunately that means it wasn't the best car in the lot. I wish I could have bought something nicer, but I did what I could."

He nods, drags his finger across the hood like he's looking for dust on my baseboards.

Come on in, Officer, you'll find plenty of dust to drag your finger through in here.

"And where were you two last night?" The question is loaded, but the way he asks it is so casual that I almost feel myself relax, but then I remember what he's doing here, why he's asking it, and I stiffen.

"Home." I cross my arms on my chest and lean against the doorframe. The welcome mat sounds scrubby and rough under my boots. Even though the sun isn't fully in the sky yet, it feels like the temperature has gone up ten degrees since I took my coffee out into the backyard.

"Home. All night?"

Dave doesn't audibly inhale, but I swear I still feel him draw a breath. As much as I'm tempted to look behind me and see the expression on his face, I keep my eyes on the officer instead. I've seen enough movies to know that when people start looking around at each other and making eye contact instead of answering the question, it's a clear sign they're guilty.

"It was a lazy night," I offer. *There.* Not a lie, not exactly.

But not the truth, either.

He nods. "I'm assuming, given how thick the trees are, that you didn't see anything? Or did you happen to see a car flying by on the road? Happen to see anyone driving faster than they should? Reckless? Out of control?"

"No." I try to look like I'm thinking things through. "Nothing like that. Like you said, the trees are thick. I have to be at our mailbox to even see the road, and the curves in it are so pronounced that I can't see far. When I'm indoors here, like we were last night, you can't see a thing on the road."

He stares at me, and I get the distinct feeling that he might not believe me, but why not? I haven't lied.

I can't see the road from the house. It was a quiet night here last night. I know nothing.

Sure, but do you suspect something?

"Fine. That's fine." He reaches for his hip, and I stiffen, thinking he's going to pull his gun, going to press it against my forehead—*you tell the truth right now or I'll shoot!*—but he simply takes a card from his pocket and offers it to me. "Call me if you think of anything else. If you hear any gossip. Nobody deserves to be a victim like your neighbor."

I take the card, but he doesn't let it go. We're caught in limbo, both of us holding on to the piece of paper, both of us connected by something so small, but so powerful.

"He died on the side of the road." The officer's eyes lock onto mine. "Nobody was there to help him. Nobody cared.

He was alone and scared, and wasn't it a little chilly last night?"

I nod without meaning to.

"He was cold. Lying on the rocks, half in the ditch. His old bones growing colder and stiffer, and there wasn't a damn thing he could do about it. Now, I want you to take my card. Reach out when something comes to you."

When, not *if*. As if he can read my mind, see my thoughts, and know that the only thing I'm thinking about right now is Dave.

"I'll call you," I say, my voice a whisper. "If I come up with anything. But I don't know anything right now, and I have no way of assuming I'll know something in the future. But I'll keep your card."

He finally lets it go, the strange dance we were caught in broken, and I slip the card into my back pocket. Give it a pat. It's slim, barely felt through the thick denim of my jeans, but it still feels heavy enough to weigh me down, to drown me, like I'm a mobster with my feet dipped in concrete.

Waddell gives me a tight smile. "Thank you." He glances past me at Dave. For a moment I think he is going to leave, his foot is even turned in the right direction, but he stops. Straightens out to face me again. Looks past me. "How old are you?"

Dave clears his throat. "Sixteen."

"Sixteen. You driving?"

"I am, yessir."

"You look older than sixteen."

Dave laughs, and I want to turn and grab him by the shoulders, shake him, tell him to stop laughing, to stop having any fun right now, but I keep a stupid smile on my face and stare at the officer.

"I get that a lot. I'm just really tall for my age."

"That you are. Do you play football?"

"No, sir. They keep trying to get me on the team, but I don't have a lot of interest in that."

"Good boy. Everyone thinks it's fun, getting out there and running into other boys, but you'll just rattle your brain around in your skull until it becomes mush. Stay off the field."

"I will."

The officer nods like he's satisfied with Dave's answers. He looks at me. His eyes narrow.

I feel breath catch in my throat, and I'm suddenly driven to say something, anything, that will make him leave the two of us alone, but I can't seem to form any words.

Just like I wanted, though, he turns and marches down the driveway. Overhead, a swallow spins through the air, arching back and forth as it hunts. In the bushes something shifts as Officer Waddell walks past it, but he doesn't slow down, and he doesn't look around him.

Determined. That's it. The man is determined to find whoever killed our neighbor, and I should be grateful for that. We don't want murderers walking around free, don't want to entertain the idea that they might strike closer to home next time. There's always a relief when someone else gets hurt or killed, because everyone wants to protect their own family.

But the truth is that as long as a murderer is walking around free, nobody is safe. There's nothing more that you can do to protect your family but make sure whoever killed another person is locked up.

Dave moves to stand next to me. I feel his presence, huge and looming, heat from his body washing over me in waves.

I have to protect my son. That's the thought racing through my mind on repeat, over and over, a demand, a promise. A threat.

"Let's go inside." Dave puts his hand on my shoulder, and it sits there, giant and heavy, like a paw. A lion. A tiger. Something bigger than I am, something more suited to surviving any way it can.

I have to protect my son.

But what if he's the one I should be protecting others from?

7

Dave's halfway through clearing the limbs in the backyard, and I head into the house to make some lemonade. Nothing fancy, I can't afford to buy fresh lemons to squeeze my own. As much as I love the idea of being Betty Crocker, of donning a cute little strawberry-print apron and making huge pitchers of homemade lemonade, that's not possible.

I have a pitcher, but it's chipped. I have an apron, but it's worn and stained, years of spaghetti sauce marring the soft purple color. And instead of fresh lemons, I have a container of yellow powder, so sweet it makes my teeth hurt, and so full of chemicals it makes me sneeze when I accidentally breathe it in. I scoop some of this powder into my pitcher and fill it with water. The top foams up, and I stir it down, adding some ice cubes from a tray in the freezer.

I've just finished filling the tray back up and sliding it carefully into place when tires in the driveway make me turn and look out the window.

It's going to be the police, I know it.

The thought is unbidden, a storm cloud that darkens my day, but when I don't see a flashing light bar, I relax. It's an old truck, forest green, with a huge brush guard on the front. Even though the morning has been an absolute roller-coaster, I feel my spirits lift when Benji hops out of the front seat.

Abandoning the lemonade, I wipe my hands on my apron and hurry to the front door, scanning his hands for flowers. It's terrible, to expect something from another person the way I expect flowers from him, but my boyfriend never fails to deliver. He's on the road so much for work driving a truck that when we do get to see each other, it's a relief.

It's worthy of a celebration.

But he's empty-handed.

Pushing the disappointment away, I step out onto the front porch and throw myself into his arms. "Benji, I wasn't sure I'd get to see you today! How are you?"

"It's Saturday, Anne Marie." His hands are light on my back, and he gently pushes me away from him, scanning my face. "Did you forget I always come by on Saturday?"

I hadn't, but the day had been such a nightmare that I wasn't even sure what day it was. Besides, he didn't sound sure earlier in the week that he'd make it over. I shake my head. "It doesn't matter. You're here now, and I'm so happy to see you! Do you want to stay for lunch?"

"I can't." He squeezes my hand, then lets it go, stepping away from me.

Like a magnet, I'm drawn to him, and I close the gap between us, reaching out and putting my hand on his hip.

"I just made some lemonade," I say, hoping to tempt him. "Besides, what else do you have to do today? You always spend Saturdays with us when you're done driving for the week."

"I passed a bunch of cops on the road," he says, ignoring my question. "What happened?"

"Oh, it's terrible. Someone hit our neighbor while he was out walking. He died."

Benji's eyes flick to the house, then back to me. "Is Dave around?"

"Sure is." For the first time since Benji and I started dating, I'm happy to have my son around. Normally I want him to disappear so I can spend some time with my boyfriend, but he's been so kind and helpful this morning. I want to show him off. "He's outside in the back doing some yard work, but I can call him here to say hi to you."

"Don't bother." He clears his throat. "I can't stay, and I just wanted to come talk to you for a minute."

"Okay." I'm still grinning at him, like a fool. It's impossible not to. Benji is strong, with wide shoulders and thick brown hair that curls around his ears. His hands are huge, and he's the kindest man I've ever met. I've thanked my lucky stars since the day he got seated in my section at the diner.

Who knew a place called Early Bird Diner could ever lead to someone finding true love?

"You're great, Anne Marie," he says.

I'm still grinning. Who doesn't like to hear how wonderful they are?

"But I can't do this any longer. It's too much."

Still grinning, like if I hold the pose, I'll be able to convince both of us that nothing terrible is going on. "Can't do what any longer?" My hand tightens into a claw, and he winces, stepping back so my arm drops back down by my side.

"This. You and me. It's too much."

"What? No. It's just enough. I miss you during the week, but then we have a lot of fun on the weekends when you're home. I thought you liked having me as your home base to come back to. 'Home is where Anne Marie is,' remember? You told your best friend that." Heat blooms in my cheeks, and I feel stinging behind my eyes, but I refuse to cry.

"I do. You're a good home base, Anne Marie." Again he looks past me into the house. "But it's too much."

What is he talking about? I stiffen, my back straight. There's a ringing in my ears that makes it sound like everything happening is far away. "Say it."

"What?"

"Say it. I want you to look me in the eyes and tell me exactly what about this is too much for you." I slide my hand into my pocket and pinch the side of my leg as hard as I can. If I keep focused on that pain, then maybe I won't focus on the pain of what's happening with Benji right now.

"Anne Marie, don't make me do that."

"Say it!"

"It's Dave." His voice is low. Furtive. It reminds me of the first time I brought him home, how careful we both were, how hard it was to keep our voices quiet even through the touching, the kissing.

"Dave?"

He nods. "He's too much, Anne Marie. You know this. I know this. Every time we talk on the phone, it's Dave this and Dave that. I have to hear about how he almost got kicked out of school again, how rude he was, how hard he makes your life. I'm sorry he makes your life hard, but he's your son, not mine. I shouldn't have to deal with him making my life hard all the time too. And I don't want to."

I don't move. I *can't* move. This isn't happening.

"Benji," I whisper, but my hand doesn't reach for him like I want it to. It's still shoved in my pocket, my nails sinking into my flesh through the thin fabric of the pocket lining.

"Anne Marie, I'm sorry. I don't want every conversation I have with someone to be about the drama they have with their kid. And I don't want to come home after being on the road all week only to have to deal with that kid. You're a great woman, but you're just not for me."

"But he's different." Hope rises in me, and I let go of my thigh, finally reaching out for him. He's stepped back again, though, and my fingers brush through the air, useless. "Dave. He's different. I promise you, he's kinder and thoughtful. We haven't gotten into a row once."

He doesn't seem to believe me. "Since when? When was the last fight you had with your son?"

I don't want to answer. As much as I'm trying to fight them back, tears are welling up more now. One blink and they'll fall, so I force my eyes to stay open, staring at Benji even as he gets distorted and watery.

"Right. See? One or two good days doesn't mean he's different, Anne Marie."

I don't dare tell him that Dave has only been good for a morning.

"I wish you luck." He sighs, runs his hand through that impossibly thick hair of his. "I hope you can find someone to be happy with. And I hope you and Dave can really figure things out."

"We have," I say, but my words are soft, and they fall on deaf ears. Benji's already walking to his truck, taking large steps like he can't wait to put me behind him. I stare at him, then slowly sink to the porch.

His truck starts with a roar. Benji must slam down on the gas harder than necessary, because gravel spits out from the tires before the truck gets purchase and jolts backwards, shooting out to the road. I want to scream at him to make a three-point-turn in the driveway, that the road is more dangerous than we thought, that he shouldn't just back out onto it like that, but I can't move.

I can't speak.

The front door squeals open, then slams. Dave sits next to me, the entire porch shifting with a sigh as he does. He swings an arm around my shoulders.

I'm angry at him, but I still soften into his touch. I still lean into him, drawing strength from his size, his heat. *This is because of you*, I want to scream, but I don't.

Because I'm his mother. Because he's my son. Because he's finally turning into the person I've always prayed he could be, and if that means I lose Benji, then I lose Benji. I have to be okay with that.

Because I have Dave. He's different now. I know he is.

8

Saturday afternoon comes and goes, night falls, and Dave goes upstairs to bed. I sit, stiff, on the sofa in the living room, just listening for any sign that he's sneaking out. Not that he's done that in a long time. Once he realized he could just take the car and leave without me stopping him, he stopped lifting the squeaky window in his small bedroom and climbing to freedom that way.

Besides, I can't imagine he'd easily fit out through the window anymore. That was something twelve- and thirteen-year-old Dave could do. As a full-grown teenager, though, he'd find it difficult to fold his limbs and sneak through.

The thought makes me laugh. Even though the day has been a nightmare, starting with my phone conversation with Carla, then the police stopping by, and finally Benji ending things with me, I can't hold in my laughter. It bubbles out of me, and I grip my stomach, my abs aching.

"Are you okay?" There's a squeak at the top of the stairs.

As quickly as if someone had thrown cold water on me, I sober up.

"I'm fine. It's just been a long day." I pause, waiting for a response. When none comes, I continue, "Are you going to bed, Dave?"

"I'm going to shower and sleep, yeah."

"You're not going out?" Just asking the question makes me wince.

"No, I thought I'd stay home tonight."

"Great," I say, reaching over to grab the TV remote. "That's great, Dave. I'm going to turn on a movie, and if you get bored up there, you can feel free to join me."

Squeaking again. He must be shifting his weight back and forth to make the stairs squeak like that. It's a strange thought, that Dave might be nervous about something. He's been so confident for years, so in control of himself and any situation he finds himself in. I don't remember the last time it seemed like he was questioning anything.

"I'm, I'm just going to go to bed. It's been a long day."

"Sounds good," I call, finally clicking the power button. "Sleep good. Tomorrow I won't make you work so much in the yard."

No response, but I didn't really expect one. Black-and-white fuzz fills the TV screen; the soft sound of static reaches my ears. The rabbit ears on the top of our TV have tilted to the side, and I get up with a sigh to adjust them.

One day I'll have enough money to actually pay for Netflix. One day I won't drive a beater like the Camry parked in the front yard. One day...well, a lot of things will happen.

But now I believe they might actually come true. Years ago if you'd asked me if Dave would ever willingly stay home on a Saturday night instead of going out with friends, I would have laughed right in your face. But that day has come. I don't remember the last time I felt this at peace in the house, this competent as a mother.

"It's been a long road." I sigh as I sink back onto the sofa. "But if this is my reward, then it's worth it."

No Benji. But I have my son back. And what mother doesn't want that?

9

MONDAY

The Monday morning rush at the Early Bird is finally dying down, and I slip into the back room to perch on a stool and toe off my shoe. I need new ones, ones with better arch support, but they've been on the to-buy list for a while, and I don't see the purchase happening anytime soon. As long as I can sneak back here from time to time to rub out the cramps threatening to work their way up my calves, I'll be fine.

My eyes are closed, and I'm digging my thumb directly into the center of my right arch when I hear the door open and close. Dropping my foot, I sit up, trying to hide what I was doing from my boss. I'm already on thin ice having to take so much time off work to handle problems with Dave. I'm sure Richard wouldn't be thrilled to see me sitting down on the job.

"Oh, Carla, you scared me." I exhale hard as I untie my laces and shove my foot back into my shoe. "Do you need me out there?"

"No, nothing like that. I just came back to say hi." She

brushes some bleached blonde hair out of her face, tucking it expertly behind her ear. Carla has to be about my age, but she looks older. She wears heavy eyeliner that ages her, especially as she sweats and wipes her face, rubbing it out from her eyes. Where my apron hangs on my thin frame—thin partly due to stress, partly due to a poor diet—she fills out her apron.

The guests love it. They love her smile and wit and somehow ignore her dark eyeliner.

"Hi." I manage a smile before tying my shoe and standing back up. "I guess I'd better get out there."

"It's not busy yet." She tucks that same bit of hair behind her ear again. Every time she turns her head, it falls back out, and I itch to pull a bobby pin from my pocket for her. "Did the police come talk to you and Dave?"

Does the air suddenly feel thin in here? There's enough room back here to rest by yourself when you need to take a load off, but just one more person in the room makes the walls feel like they've moved in. Behind me is a rack with overflow canned goods, and a mop leans in the corner.

"Sure did. Some nice officer just asking if we knew anything, but I told him we didn't, so he left." I lift one shoulder and drop it. Even though Carla and I work together and live on the same road, there's no way I'm going to tell her about the intense fear I felt when the police showed up on my front porch.

Nobody needs to know how worried I was.

"Nothing?" She peers at me. "I really thought someone on the street would have seen something. Heard something. You know how people drive so quickly on the road."

"It's scary," I admit. "And what happened is terrible. I really hope they find whoever hit him."

"I'm sure they will." She nods like she's working hard to convince both of us. "You can't hide from your crimes, especially not in a small town. My grandaddy always said that even if you pick your nose in the fog, someone will see you."

"He's right," I say, edging past her to the door. Now, more than anything, I want to get out of here. "I'd better head back out there in case a customer needs me. I'm on thin ice as it is because I've had to call in a few times to help out with Dave's school stuff."

"Is he still getting in trouble?" Carla's right on my heels as I leave the room. She pauses just long enough to close the door behind us, then keeps talking. "I know for a while he was having difficulty, but you got that straightened out, right? I'd hate to see you lose your job."

I grit my teeth. Why is it always the people you don't want to be around the ones who are determined to stay as close to you as possible? "Dave's wonderful," I say, and for the first time in a while I don't feel like I'm lying. "We spent a great weekend at home together, and he got a lot of work in the yard done for me."

She smiles, showing more of her teeth than feels necessary. "I'm really glad to hear things are going well with him. I know teenage boys can be such a handful."

"Sure can," I say, because what else is there to do? She knows I've had trouble with Dave. Denying it would only make her suspicious and make me out to be a liar. "But they all calm down eventually. Seems to me like Dave has finally hit that point in his life where he doesn't want to be as wild as he once was."

"That's nice." She pats her apron pocket, then pulls a notepad out, flourishing it in front of my face like I don't have an exact replica in my front pocket. "Anyway, off to make some tips. Gotta keep them coming in." She adjusts her top, showing off more cleavage than I'd be comfortable with, then sweeps away into the dining section. The sound of chatting diners reaches my ears, and I roll my shoulders back.

Time to get to work. Even though things calmed down with Dave over the weekend, I still want to be on guard. The last thing I need is for everything to come crashing down around my head right when I thought things were better. If it does, I'll have to be prepared. There's no way my boss will allow me to keep working if I have to miss one more scheduled shift because of Dave's antics at school.

Nerves ripple through me, and I check my phone just in case I've missed a call or text from his school, but there's nothing. No calls, no texts. No emails, either.

No matter. I push the thought of what my son might be getting into at school from my mind and slip the phone back into my pocket. Time to focus on my shift. I'm not going to let myself think about how strange Carla was acting. I'm also not going to let myself worry about the other shoe dropping with Dave.

People can change. And sure, there's usually an inciting incident to make that happen, but thinking about it will only make me nervous.

Because if I'm being honest with myself, Dave's behavior changed right around the time our neighbor was killed. But that has to be a coincidence. I refuse to think it could be anything more.

10

WEDNESDAY

Wednesday night is bingo night, and even though I know how old that makes me sound, there's something about getting out of the house, getting to talk to new people, and the chance of winning some money that makes me feel alive. It's silly, to want to dress up for something like this when I know I'm going to be one of the youngest people there, but after Benji ended things with me...well, I just want to feel better.

Turning, I look at myself in the rectangular mirror I hung behind my bedroom door. I have on a blue dress that falls to my knees as well as gold sandals. The sandals have seen better days, but once I'm sitting at a table, nobody will be looking at my feet. After washing my hair, I put some curlers in it to dry, and now I fluff it some, raking my fingers through the curls to make them look a bit more natural.

Jewelry. There's one particular pair of earrings I have, ones that were my mother's, and while I only wear them from time to time, they're special to me. They're also diamonds and the most expensive things I own. I've come close to feeling like I had to sell them a few times, but I've always managed to hang on to them.

I keep them in a small velvet pouch at the bottom of my jewelry box. Everything else in the box is fake, but the earrings? They're real. Sometimes I pull them out for church. And I know it's just me being funny, but I love wearing them to our street picnics. Everyone always compliments me on them. Even with jeans and a casual top, they make me feel like a million bucks.

Inspiring envy in other people is probably a sin, but I can't help it. Sometimes I want people to look at me and want what I have.

Pushing aside a macaroni necklace Dave made me when he was little and didn't hate going to school, I frown. The little blue velvet bag isn't in here.

A quick glance at my watch assures me that I have some time before I need to leave, so I take a deep breath and start from the top, slowly digging through the layers of jewelry. The long necklaces are going to get tangled up if I'm not careful, but I don't care right now.

I want my earrings.

There's a knock on my door, and I step back out of the way so Dave can enter.

He frowns, watching my frantic movements. "What are you doing?"

"I can't find my earrings." Frustrated now, I take the jewelry box to my bed and upend it on the comforter. I know I should be methodical about this, but I need those earrings. "I wanted to wear them tonight, and I can't find them."

"You wanted to wear them to bingo?"

I frown, pausing long enough to glance at him. "Is that a problem?"

"No, I just wouldn't think you'd want to wear them there. Aren't they a little fancy for that?"

I exhale hard, suddenly hot and sweaty. Tendrils of hair stick to the back of my neck. It's not just the frustration of how Dave is talking to me right now that's making my skin feel hot and sticky, it's also the fact I'm annoyed that I can't find the earrings. They're my favorite, and I always make sure to put them right back in their little bag and then at the bottom of my jewelry box after I've worn them.

"I don't care if they're too fancy," I say, and I realize I'm speaking through gritted teeth. It makes my jaw ache, and I force myself to relax my muscles. "I wanted to wear them, they make me feel good, and I'm frustrated that I can't find them." I pause, not wanting to allow myself to think the one thought pressing at the back of my mind. "Have you seen them?"

He pauses, just a beat, but it's a beat too long. Then again, wouldn't I have become just as suspicious if he had immediately brushed off my concern?

"I haven't seen them. Sorry you can't find them." Another pause, during which I force myself to look at him. "Are you still going to go?"

His face is perfectly smooth. His hands, which are already so big he can easily palm a basketball, flex at his sides. I watch their movement until he realizes what I'm doing and shoves his hands in his pockets; then I drag my gaze up to his eyes.

"I'm still going to go," I say, searching his expression for any emotion. Guilt, maybe? The fact that that's what I'm looking for makes my stomach twist.

"Okay, good. Good. I hope you have fun." He gives a little shrug that makes him look a lot younger than he is.

That's one of the problems we've run into time and time again with his teachers and school administrators. Dave is a big kid, much bigger than some of the teachers at the high school, even. It's almost impossible for any adult to look at a sixteen-year-old the size of my son and not have higher expectations.

They expect him to be smarter than he is. More well behaved. They expect his manners to be impeccable and then get frustrated when he's just a normal kid.

"I will have fun," I say, the words automatic. When was the last time he was still at the house when I went out to bingo? He's always gone, often fighting with me about who's going to take the car, but not recently. Not since...

No. I'm not going to think about that.

"Okay." He gives me a small smile. "Sorry about your earrings, Mom." Then he's gone, thumping down the hall to his bedroom.

From my vantage point by the bed, I can see his door open and then shut. He doesn't slam it, which is how he normally operates. Loud. In control. Making sure everyone else is aware that he's there and of how he's feeling.

But I hardly register the fact that he doesn't slam his door. I barely pay attention to the way he turns on his music, much softer than normal. It's not the pounding bass that I'm so used to, not the loud music that makes me take a Tylenol and press some little moldable earplugs into my ears.

Nope. None of that.

The only thing I can think about is what he said to me right before he left.

Sorry about your earrings, Mom.

Not *I'm sorry you lost them.* Or *I hope you find them.*

No.

Sorry about your earrings.

It wasn't an admission of guilt. I won't go that far. But it was an apology.

And Dave never apologizes. I can't remember the last time he took responsibility for his actions or tried to shield me from what he'd done. This is uncharted territory for me, and I can't help the fact that my knees suddenly feel like they're going to give out.

Slowly, I turn. Sit on the edge of the bed. I rest my face in my hands and force myself to take a few deep breaths to try to calm down. Think clearer.

Something with Dave has changed.

Sorry about your earrings, Mom.

"Oh God," I whisper, pressing my fingers hard into my temples. That doesn't stop the pounding already building, and I adjust, digging my fingernails into the thin, sensitive skin there, hoping for pain that will be bright enough, sharp enough, to make me snap out of what I'm thinking.

Because it's not just about the earrings, is it?

I'm not stupid. Mothers aren't stupid. We might not want to see what's right in our faces because we choose not to see something terrible, not because we don't know what's happening. We don't want to admit it.

Dave apologized for the earrings. Anyone who wasn't his mother might take that at face value. They might accept his words as him just being kind, of him telling me that he feels bad that they're missing, that I can't find them, that I'm letting this worry over my earrings overshadow the fun I want to have tonight.

But I'm his mother. He wasn't just apologizing for the

missing earrings, was he? He doesn't feel bad for me because I lost them. He feels bad because he took them.

And I think he feels bad about even more than that.

11

THURSDAY

This time I don't wait for the secretary to thumb behind her and tell me the principal is waiting. I'm in a hurry, on lunch break from work, and if I don't get through this meeting as quickly as possible and back to the Early Bird before Richard catches on that I'm not there, then I'm in trouble.

"Ms. Kerns, thanks for making some time to talk to me." Mrs. Byler has a huge salad on her desk, and she pushes it out of the way, but not before I notice that it's loaded with grilled chicken, fresh veggies, with dressing on the side. *Monster. Who doesn't slather ranch all over everything?*

"Of course. I'm glad we could make it work during my lunch break, but I really don't have a lot of time." To reinforce this, I glance at my watch.

"This won't take long. I wanted to let you know that I've filled out the paperwork to have Dave transferred to the remedial high school." She pauses, letting that sink in, then continues, "I know you were in last week, and we spoke, but—"

"No." I plant my hand on her desk and shake my head. "No, you told me he had another chance. You can't spring this on me like this, not out of nowhere, not when he hasn't done anything wrong."

"You didn't let me finish." Her mouth is pressed into a firm line. "I filled out the paperwork and sent it to the county to have it processed after what happened on Friday."

My mouth goes dry. "Friday?"

"He was smoking after school in the parking lot." A smile curls the edges of her mouth. "My hands are tied."

"You can't do this," I say, leaning forward. Desperation weighs heavy on me. "Dave has turned a new leaf, I promise you he has. And smoking after school isn't enough to get him expelled."

"That's what the board of education just told me." She drops her hand on a piece of paper I hadn't noticed before. "Also, the remedial school is full. No more students."

I sigh with relief.

"Have you considered homeschooling him?" She steeples her fingers and peers at me like one might look at an interesting insect.

"Homeschool? No. I work full time. There's no way I could do that and keep my job."

"I just think Dave would thrive in another environment. He's...well, he's so *big*." She looks at me imploringly like she wants me to agree. "And it's a bit of a *Of Mice and Men* situation with him sometimes."

"What does that mean?"

"Nothing. I just don't think our school is the best option for Dave. If there were anywhere else..."

"There isn't. I can't homeschool him, and your attempts to have him removed from your school have failed." I feel feral, like I'm backed into a corner, and I bare my teeth in a smile. "He has a right to free education."

She sighs. "He does, yes."

"Mrs. Byler." I shift, sitting straight up. "What was the point of this meeting? To make me feel bad that I can't homeschool him? To tell me you tried to get rid of him but couldn't? Or just to insult him? I've read Steinbeck."

She has the grace to blush but covers it up with a laugh. "I want him to start seeing the school counselor. We discussed the possibility before, and you shot it down, but I think it's the best option for Dave."

"And you only have his best interests at heart."

She puts her hand on her chest like I've wounded her. "Of course. It's just that some kids are followers, and some are leaders. You can't turn followers into leaders, but you can teach them how to stand on their own two feet. I think that's what Dave needs."

"Right." I glance at my watch. As much as I'd love to sit here and argue this with Mrs. Byler some more, I'm running out of time to get back to work. I'm going to have to run as it is. "Send me the papers to sign, and I'll look at them. I'll consider it."

She stands, nodding. "I can get them right now. Just give me a minute."

"I don't have a minute." I stand too, leaning over her desk just a bit. I'm so hungry, having skipped breakfast, that I feel a little woozy, but I'm not going to let her see that. "Next time you want to insult my son, don't. I know you don't like Dave, Mrs. Byler, but you need to give him a chance. He's changed. For the better."

She holds my gaze. "Oh, he's changed, has he?" Her words have a bite that wasn't there before. "Then I guess he won't be intimidating people or smoking or drinking or skipping class ever again?"

"Watch and see." I glare at her. "I've got it under control. Send the papers if that's the path you think we need to take. But threaten my son again and I promise you, you won't be the only person reaching out to the school board."

Can she tell how nervous I am? I hope she can't see how I'm breaking into a sweat, how my cheeks feel flushed and hot. I keep my hands planted on her desk because I'm afraid that if I lift them, they'll start shaking.

I can't have that.

"You certainly are a devoted mother," she remarks, but there's no admiration in her voice. "Not every parent would go to bat for their child like you have. Sounds like you're willing to do just about anything."

"Just about." My teeth are gritted as I walk to the door. "You have a good rest of your day."

"Oh, you too. I'll be in touch if anything changes around here with Dave's behavior. Fingers crossed he stays on the straight and narrow." To prove her point, she crosses fingers on both hands and holds them up in the air for me to see.

"Fingers crossed," I parrot back; then I close her office door behind me. Sagging against it, I check my watch.

Five minutes to get back to the diner. This meeting was an absolute waste of time, and if I lose my job because of it, I'm going to scream. My feet ache, but I hurry down the tiled hall, ignoring students who step out of my way, then burst out into the open air.

If I run, I can make it. Leaving my car at the diner so Richard wouldn't know I'd left work seemed like a good idea at the time, but I'm going to have to push it. I'm halfway to the diner when my phone rings. Without breaking my stride,

I push the green button to answer and press it against my ear.

“Hello?” There’s a stitch in my side, and I grab it with my free hand, squeezing tight like that’s going to be enough to make the pain disappear.

“Anne Marie.” Richard’s voice has a knife edge to it. “Where the hell are you?”

12

"I'm so sorry," I say, the apology falling from my lips before I've even fully entered Richard's office. I feel like a kid who just got caught smoking behind the auditorium at school.

Richard's staring at something on his computer, but he slowly looks up at me, one eyebrow raised, his fingers drumming on the desk. "Where were you?"

I wince. "The high school," I admit, "but not because Dave was in trouble. Things have changed, Richard, and his principal called me in to tell me how amazing he's been doing. I don't know why she didn't just do it over the phone, but she wanted to talk to me. I won't have to go back anytime soon."

"Give me your apron." He stands, holding out one hand. His fingers are meaty, thick sausage fingers, and I stare at them for a moment before what he just said hits me.

"No." I hate this apron, hate what it represents—that I'll never have a better job or be more than I am right now—but it's the only thing standing between me and absolute failure. "Richard, please. Don't do this."

"I warned you, Anne Marie. I told you that if you couldn't keep your personal life from getting in the way at work, this wasn't the place for you. I don't think you believed me, but maybe you will now. Apron." He snaps his fingers.

Tears bubble up behind my eyes. "Richard," I say, doing everything I can to remain calm, "please. Today was an accident. I didn't think I had a choice, and my lunch break isn't technically up for another minute. I made it back in time, the same time that I would have otherwise just been sitting in the back room eating a sandwich." My stomach growls at the thought.

"It's the principle." His hand hasn't wavered.

My fingers are twisted in my apron strings, and I glance from his unmoving hand up to his face.

His glare hasn't wavered, either.

"Okay," I say, my tongue thick. I don't want to admit defeat, and I certainly don't want to give in to Richard when it means losing everything I've worked so hard for, but I don't see that I have another choice. I don't see any other way out of this besides just giving him what he wants, no matter what that means for me.

But first I'll have to untie my apron. My fingers ache in the strings but don't want to respond when I tell them to move.

"Anne Marie, thank goodness you're off lunch." Carla leans in the door, gasping like she just ran a marathon. "I'm so sorry to bug you, Richard, but we're slammed, and the three tables that just arrived asked specifically for Anne Marie." Pink spreads from her ample cleavage up her neck as she looks at our boss. "I need her."

"She needs me," I whisper. My fingers hurt like the apron strings are cutting off circulation to my fingertips, but I don't dare look down at them. "Please, Richard. I need this job. You need me."

"You're replaceable."

"They want Anne Marie." Carla steps forward, resting her hand on my lower back. "What do you want me to say to them, Richard?"

He stares at me. The disgust in his eyes is evident. "Anne Marie," he begins, but Carla cuts him off.

"I can't finish out this shift on my own, Richard. When in the world will you be able to hire someone else and get them trained?" She sounds desperate, but my eyes are locked on Richard's face, and I don't turn to look at her.

Slowly, his hand lowers. Lands on the desk. He leans forward, supporting his weight on it as his eyes search mine. "I need you right now, but I don't have to keep you on. Remember that, Anne Marie. You're replaceable."

"I'll remember that," I tell him, like it's not something I already think about every single day. But he didn't fire me, not yet, and I give him a small nod before scurrying out of the office after Carla.

"Thank you," I tell her, once we're in the main dining area. "Seriously, he was about to can me." I look around at the tables, half of which are empty; then I arch an eyebrow at her. No way did she need me out here. And in all my years of working here, I've never had a customer ask specifically for me.

She shrugs, obviously aware of what I'm thinking. "What's one lie between friends? As long as things work out the way we want them to, does it really matter?"

"No," I say, and while I am grateful that she went to bat

for me, something about lying to Richard doesn't feel great. I guess I have to consider the alternative, that I could very easily have just lost my job.

"Great, I'm glad you agree. Besides, that man is incredibly lazy. You and I both know he'll threaten to fire you as many times as he can, but he doesn't actually want to go to the effort of finding and hiring someone new. If he put time into actually running this place, then he wouldn't be able to just sit in his office munching on stale donuts and watching reruns of *Law and Order*. Now that that's done, let's make some tips." She grins. "Just remember that I went out on a limb for you, okay? When Richard was looking for you, I couldn't very well hide that you were gone. But I just lied to him for you. That's not nothing."

"I'll remember." My apron strings are loose from me yanking on them, and I re-tie them quickly before pulling my pad of paper from my pocket and walking to the nearest table. "Thanks, Carla," I say, over my shoulder.

"Anytime, darling. I have your back; you have mine. Remember that."

I'll remember that, alright. What I don't like, though, is how much that feels like a threat.

13

Dave's already home, tucked up in his room, listening to music, by the time I get off work and drive back to the house. I hear him upstairs, hear the strains of some rock band I don't know, but I ignore it while making dinner. Hamburger Helper tonight—*again*—which certainly won't win me any awards in the kitchen, but it's cheap and easy and filling.

"Dinner," I call, when I have two huge bowls of the stuff ready to go. It smells vaguely fake, like the cheese sauce isn't really made from milk, but I'm not going to look at the box. Sometimes ignorance really is bliss. "Dave, dinner!"

Nothing. The music still pounds through the house, but Dave doesn't come down. Maybe he hasn't heard me. I cast a glance at the table where the two bowls are steaming, then grab the handrail and head upstairs. He's probably on his bed, his eyes closed, transported to somewhere—anywhere but here—thanks to his music.

"Dave." I knock three times on his door. "Dinnertime, Dave. Can you turn off the music and come on out?"

Nothing.

I close my eyes and lean my forehead against his door. Anxiety wraps its fingers around my throat. How many times have I gone through these motions with him before? Me looking for him, him either ignoring me or having already snuck out somewhere?

But I really thought we'd turned a corner this time. I really thought...well, it doesn't matter what I thought, does it? Not if we're back to square one.

"Dave, I'm coming in!" My heart catches in my throat as I turn the doorknob because I'm expecting it to be locked, to refuse to open. For just a moment I feel frozen in time; then I'm tipping forward and stepping into his room.

The music wraps around me, a thick fog. His lights are on, his window open. A cool breeze flits through, lifting the curtains. Dave's room is always messy, always full of things I keep thinking belong elsewhere in the house, and today is no different.

He has a desk in the corner that boasts three empty bowls from him bringing cereal upstairs. The surface is empty otherwise, leading me to believe that he never actually uses it for homework. Piles of clothes are scattered around the floor, and his bed is unmade. There's a red rug in the middle of the room, and that's where Dave sits, leaning back against his bed, his eyes closed, a piece of paper clutched in his hand.

"Dave, are you okay?" I hurry to him, then fall on my knees next to him. He's pale, unmoving. Reaching out, I lightly rest the back of my hand on his forehead. Does he have a fever? Do I need to call an ambulance? "Are you okay?"

No fever. He finally opens his eyes and heaves a sigh. I

think for sure he's going to yell at me for coming into his room without permission, but his lip trembles. He bites it, then gives his head a shake.

"Hang on," I tell him, standing and hurrying to his stereo. All of the bands he listens to have the most ridiculous names, and I don't recognize any of them. The man currently screaming at me is enough to make me want to pull out my hair.

I click the knob to turn off the music, and the silence that falls is almost painful. For a moment, I stare at the pack of cigarettes next to the stereo, wondering where Dave got them; then I remember that it doesn't really matter and hurry back to my son.

"Okay, I can think now," I tell him, taking one of his hands in mine. His fingers are freezing. I massage them, trying to warm him up. "Dave, tell me what's going on. Something happened. What is it?"

He shakes his head. A single tear streams down his cheek, and I feel something painful twist deep inside me. This is my son, the one person I swore I would protect with my life. Yes, we've had a difficult path up until now, but that's what the world does to you. It brings pain. It's a dark, ugly world, and it will make you ugly too if you're not careful.

When he doesn't answer, I wipe the tear from his cheek. "Let me see this paper, Dave," I say, gently tugging it from him. He resists at first, then lets go, letting me pluck the paper from his grip.

I read it once, then again. Every word on the paper is angry, dark. I felt sick to my stomach before, but now I truly feel like I might throw up.

"Where did you get this?"

He shakes his head. "I can't tell you."

"Dave, this is important." I reach behind him and put the letter on the bed. My hands shake, and I have to resist the urge to rip it up, to scatter the pieces, to flush them down the toilet or throw them into the wind. "Dave, you need to tell me exactly what's going on. I can't help you if you don't tell me the truth."

This is big. *Huge.* It's much bigger than anything I've ever dealt with before, and I need my son to see that. I need him to understand that he can't just shake his head, brush this under the rug, forget about it until another time. This is something the two of us need to deal with. Now.

"Is it a joke?" I'm pleading. The note of fear in my voice makes me hate myself, but I can't help it. "Dave, is it a joke from one of your friends? Did they think this was funny?"

He doesn't move. I've watched movies where people go catatonic, where they completely stop responding to outside stimuli. I always thought it was a joke, something made up for the big screen, but even if that's not what's happening here, there's some truth to it.

My heart hammers. My skin feels clammy. Sweat breaks out on my brow, but I don't move to wipe it away. Where I had been so hungry before, just the thought of food now makes me feel sick.

"Look me in the eyes and tell me this is a joke," I command, grabbing my son by the chin and twisting his head to look at me. He screws his eyes shut, his chest rising and falling. It's only when I squeeze his chin hard, my fingers sinking into his flesh, that he finally looks at me.

"It's not a joke."

Not a joke.

Three little words slam into my chest and almost knock

me backward. I fight to stay crouched on my heels, not to fall back flat on the floor as I stare at him in shock.

"Is this the first note?" Leaning forward, I grab it and wave it in front of his face. Like he doesn't know exactly what it says. Like he doesn't have it memorized, like those words aren't marching through his veins right now, becoming a refrain that only he can hear.

"No."

"The first was...what?"

I stare at the note while I wait for Dave to respond.

Remember that I'm watching you.

Who would write that? And why in the world would someone give that to my son? Why are they watching him? And who is it from?

He mumbles something.

"I'm sorry," I snap, looking up at him. "I missed that. Say it again."

"Your earrings."

"My...earrings?" I'm shocked, but should I be? Of course, my earrings. That's why he didn't seem surprised they were gone; that's why he apologized. That's why I couldn't find them.

"I'm sorry. The first note, they wanted your earrings. So I took them. I had to. I thought it would stop it, but this note was here today, and now I don't know what to do." More mumbling.

Ice trickles down my back. I want to go back in time, turn the radio back on, sit down at the kitchen table, and stuff my mouth full of Hamburger Helper. I want to pretend none of this is happening. I need to undo it all, and I don't know how.

That's the worst part. In all my years of living on this earth, of going along behind Dave and picking up his mess, of trying to be the best mother I can be, I don't know how to undo this.

How to fix it.

"They sent the note because—"

I clap a hand over his mouth. I don't want to hear what he's going to say. I don't *need* to hear it.

Because I already know it. I know why someone would send him blackmail notes.

I know what he did.

14

Our dinner sits on the counter, the sauce, pasta, and meat slowly cooling and congealing into a mess I'm sure I'm going to throw away later rather than eat. Wasting food isn't something Dave and I have the luxury of doing, but there's no way I'm going to be able to eat Hamburger Helper ever again without remembering this night.

This moment.

The moment I found out what my son did.

"Start from the beginning," I say. We both have a cup of coffee in our hands. The mug is so hot my nerves scream for me to let it go, to cool off my skin, but I can't seem to move. The pain is the only thing keeping me grounded right now, the only thing keeping me from absolutely losing it.

"It was Friday night," he says, swallowing hard. "I was out with friends and came home."

Silence.

"Were you drinking?"

He nods.

"A lot?"

This makes him look up at me. "Does it matter?"

"No, I guess it doesn't. What happened?"

"I didn't see him. George. He wasn't there, and then he was."

"Where? In front of his house?"

He shakes his head. "No, out by the main road, where Grace Road tees into it. I made the turn coming home, and then he was there."

"And you hit him?" I squeeze the mug tighter, suck in tiny gasps of air. My lungs feel like they're about to collapse, like I can't fill them enough to catch my breath. Behind me, at the kitchen window, a fly buzzes, slamming into the glass over and over in a desperate bid to escape.

I feel the same way.

"I just kept driving," he says, closing his eyes. "I didn't know what to do. I came home. Parked the car. Took a shower."

I nod. Even though I was in bed Friday night while all this was going on, I'd been vaguely aware of him coming home. I'd heard him moving around, heard the shower click on and then off. It was only then, when I thought he was home safe, that I allowed myself to fall asleep.

"You said there was a first note." I hate prodding him to continue, but he has to keep talking. He has to fill in the gaps.

"I came downstairs to check the car. Look for...a dent, I guess. Hair. Blood. I don't know." He shrugs, sighs. "And it was there, right on the front porch. On the welcome mat."

"What did it say?"

"It said that they saw me. That they knew what I'd done. That he was dead, and it was on me to follow instructions, or they would tell the police. It said to bring your earrings to the park and leave them by the bench. That they'd come pick them up." He looks up at me, his eyes haunted. "I thought that would end it."

"Why didn't you come to me?" I reach for his hand but don't touch him. The dark expression on his face scares me.

"Because I didn't know what you'd do! Because everyone thinks I'm a terrible person, and I guess I am, aren't I? I killed him, and I ran, and now someone knows the truth. What would you have done, Mom?"

"I don't know, but we'll figure it out. I promise you, Dave, I'm not going to leave you to handle this on your own." Now I do grab his hand. I link our fingers together. Squeeze.

"They're not going to stop." His voice is hollow. "I thought they just wanted the earrings, that stealing them would put an end to it, but it didn't. Why would they reach out again? What if they want more from me, things I can't give them?"

I don't answer. The hollow feeling in my stomach is growing, slowly taking over. I feel like I'm about to tip into it, fall into a void that I can't get back out of.

My son killed someone.

I take those four words and turn them over and over my mind, trying my best to make them make sense.

My son is a murderer.

That's clearer, but still difficult for me to comprehend, for me to wrap my mind around. Turning, I look over my shoulder, around the living room. Surely this is a joke, some sick prank, some final nail in the coffin of our relationship.

But when I let my gaze fall back on Dave, when I see the torment in his eyes, I know it's not a joke.

"They'll stop," I say, and I'm pleased that my voice sounds firm. I sound confident. Inside, I'm shriveling up, but on the outside I puff out my chest, straighten up in my seat. I squeeze his fingers and nod. "They'll stop."

"You don't know that," he whispers. "We don't even know who they are."

He's right. I've been thinking of this person, this...blackmailer, as a nebulous entity in a cloak with a hood. In my mind it's just someone in the shadows, someone impossible to see, impossible to touch. But they're real. They know what my son did. And he's right—why would they willingly back down?

Unless I make them. But I'd have to find them first.

"Mom, are you mad?"

His anguish squeezes my heart, and I'm thrown back in time a decade, to when he was just starting kindergarten and came home filthy from a scrap on the playground. He'd been so worried I would get upset, more worried about that than anything else, if I'm honest.

I lock eyes with him. If I squint a little, use my imagination, I can still picture my little boy. It's getting harder with every passing year. Of course he doesn't look exactly the same. And he doesn't wear the same clothes. He's grown out of some of his mannerisms, the ones that I found so endearing when he was a little kid.

But he's still my little boy. No matter what he's done, Dave is still my little boy.

"I don't know if I can fix this," I say, choking out the words.

Dave blinks at me like he can't believe what I'm saying.

"I'm not mad, but I wish you'd come to me sooner, come to me that night. Maybe we could have stopped this person. We'll get them off our backs."

"But the note—"

I hold up my hand to cut him off. "They'll get bored, Dave. You gave them my earrings, but what else do we have?" I have to fight against the mental image of my son sneaking into my bedroom, digging through my jewelry box, taking my earrings, and then giving them to...someone, I don't know who.

Just the thought of him doing that, of him breaking my trust, makes me feel sick.

"I thought the earrings would be enough to make them leave me alone," he repeats, but I'm barely listening to him now. "I thought they'd back off. What if I keep getting notes like this for the rest of my life?"

"Or they get tired of their little games and call the police," I say. I'm not really thinking about the words that leave my lips. They just slip out, and Dave looks horrified.

"We have to find them." He stands, pushing his chair back from the table. It squeals against the floor, and I wince, but he doesn't seem to notice. "We have to figure out who sent this and take care of them."

I'm already shaking my head. "There's no way to do that, Dave, and if you'd calm down a little and think straight, I'm sure you'd know that, too. They know who you are, but you don't know who they are."

"We'll figure it out." He's breathing hard, his chest rising and falling rapidly. "We'll figure it out, Mom. We'll stop them."

"Or maybe this is it." I stand, too, unwilling to let him

tower over me. Even when I draw myself up to my full height, he's still taller. He looms over me. "Did you ever think that, Dave? Maybe they know there's not much more to be had from us. They got the earrings. What more can they take?" I gesture around the kitchen, hopelessness almost choking me.

"I don't know." He glowers at me. "But some people won't ever stop."

Look in a mirror, Dave.

"You have to be on your best behavior," I tell him. "You know that, don't you? No messing up at school or at home. No speeding. No breaking the law."

It hits me that this is why he's been so good. It's not because I'm finally getting through to him, not because he's starting to listen to me, starting to realize that I'm a good influence, that I'm someone he should pay attention to. It's because he was scared half to death.

"I'm behaving." He sucks in a breath, then slams his hand down on the table. Hot coffee sloshes up and over the rim of my mug, but neither one of us move to clean it up. "I'm behaving, haven't you noticed?"

"I have noticed." I long to hug him, to feel him in my arms, so I step around the table and do just that, resting my cheek against his chest. "You've been so good. You just have to keep it up."

His movements feel robotic as he reaches up and pats me on the back, but I don't mind. I don't mind if he's returning the hug out of guilt or shame or fear. The fact he's hugging me at all makes this all worth it.

Dave can do this. He can be better, stay on the straight and narrow, show this blackmailer that he's a better person. Yes, he killed someone.

But it was an accident.

And as much as I hate to admit it, even to myself, but if that's what it takes for me to get my son back, it was worth it. I've enjoyed the Dave I've had for the past few days.

I'm not going to let this blackmailer take him from me.

15

FRIDAY

We're both on tenterhooks in the morning, each of us dancing around the other like we're afraid of making the wrong move, of the house orchestra screeching to a halt, of the other person figuring out that we don't, in fact, know the choreography. Now we sit opposite each other, both of us trying to pretend like breakfast is normal.

I stayed home last night, too afraid of whoever might be watching my little family to leave the house. It felt strange, Dave and myself stuck in the house together, each one of us lost in our own thoughts, both of us unwilling to go anywhere.

If George had been killed right by his driveway, then the list of suspects blackmailing us would be smaller. I think Dave and I could figure it out, slowly working our way down the list, coming up with the name of the person daring enough to threaten my son. To threaten me.

But George was killed at the end of the road, right where it meets a main road that runs through the heart of our small town like an artery. There's not a lot of traffic on it at night, but there's enough to make it impossible for us to pinpoint who saw the incident.

But someone did. Someone saw Dave, then followed him down the road to our house, watching as he turned on downstairs lights before making his way up to the bathroom, watching as I finally turned off my reading lamp and rolled over to go to sleep.

And what if guilt hadn't driven Dave to go outside and check the car? I might have been the one to find the note in the morning. If I had, if I could go back in time and find it first, maybe I could have put an end to this before it really ramped up. I could have stopped it, maybe found out who the blackmailer was before Dave knew about them, and then...

What?

Kill them?

The thought chills me, and I still, holding a fork halfway to my mouth.

"Mom? You okay?" Dave's right there—just like he has been all morning. He's hovering, almost like he's afraid to let me out of his sight.

"I'm fine," I say, forcing a smile. "Just realized that we need to get a move on if I'm going to make it to work and you're going to make it to school. I can give you a ride."

The thought of driving the car that hit someone—that killed someone—makes me feel sick.

A pause. Then, "That would be great. Thanks."

"Good. Great." I have a goal now, and that makes it easier for me to finish my breakfast. I shovel it in, careful not to spill any down the front of my apron. Richard hates it when people come to work messy. During my first month at Early

Bird, he would make me stand still in front of him while he circled around me like a predator. It was only after he'd determined that I was dressed appropriately and pristine that he'd let me grab my notepad and start taking orders.

That's over, thank goodness, but I'm not about to give him any reason to do it again. It was humiliating.

We finish breakfast and clean up the kitchen in silence. Dave pounds up the stairs to get his backpack, and I grab my keys and cell phone, slipping the latter into my pocket while I wait for him. There's a lot of thunking coming from upstairs, and I do my best to ignore it.

Before, I'd want to know what he was doing. I'd be curious, which I think is normal for a mother. But now that the worst thing ever has happened, I can't really care. I don't know what Dave is doing up there, but he's not out driving.

He's not out there killing another person.

A shiver rocks over me, and I hurry outside to step into the sun. I hate cold chills, like someone has walked over my grave, like a terrible thing is going to happen and I just don't know it yet. Outside, the birds are singing. There are some puffy white clouds in the sky, some of them hanging so low it's easy to imagine that I could just lift my hand up and touch them.

From inside, I hear Dave pounding down the stairs, but my attention is focused on the road. Someone's driving down it, gravel kicking back. The crunch of gravel carries through the still morning air.

Lifting my hand, I shield my eyes from the sun as I wait for the driver to keep going. The crunching slows, and my heart picks up the pace, hammering away in my chest like it's trying to break through my ribs.

A flash of light as the car noses its way up my driveway. I

still haven't moved, am still standing on the porch in my apron, waiting to get the day started.

Police. The thought hits me, fast and unbidden, and I swallow hard, fighting down bile.

But unless it's a detective in an unmarked car, it's not the police. There's no light bar flashing blue, no searchlight on the side of the vehicle. It's a Prius, light blue, and it hums to a stop next to my Camry before the driver kills the engine.

"Mom?" Dave's at my side. He puts his hand on my lower back, and I shift closer to him, grateful that he's here. Before, he had a secret, but he was the only one who knew it. I didn't have to worry about keeping it.

It's worse, knowing about it, knowing what he did. But we're a united front, and there isn't anything that can break us.

"A friend of yours?" I ask as the door swings open and a stocky man in a wrinkled button-up shirt and chinos steps out. He wipes his forehead, then catches us watching him and throws us a wave.

Like twins, Dave and I lift our hands in response.

"Never seen him before." Dave shifts a little, his other hand still on my lower back. "But we don't really have time to stand around and talk."

He's right. "Can I help you?" I ask, walking away from the house to meet him by his car. A strange man showing up on my property? It's never a good sign, and I don't want him to think he'll be invited in.

"I'm Nate Mullinax," he says, extending a beefy hand to me. "From WTZQ. I wanted to swing by, see if you or your" —he glances past me, looks at Dave— "son," he says, obviously having spotted the backpack, "know anything about what happened to your neighbor."

"You're not police?" Dave talks quickly, like words are on a conveyor belt. I've lived in the South long enough to expect words to be slower, to rely on a more relaxed cadence. He steps away from me, his eyes locked on the man.

"Not police, no." I haven't shaken his hand, and he shoves it in his pocket. "I'm from the news. I'm writing a story on—"

"We don't have anything to say," I tell him, cutting him off. "It's a tragedy, but neither of us know anything. And you're stopping us from being on time for work and school, so I need you to leave."

He stares at me. "The last thing I want is to be in your way, ma'am, but I really could use your help on this story. You see—"

"We're on our way out." Dave's next to me again. "Did you not hear my mom? I can't be late to school."

The reporter has to tilt his head back to look Dave in the face. "A man was killed," he says, giving a little nod like he's found his soapbox and is standing firm. "A man was killed, and while the police are looking for the killer, I don't think we should focus so much on that person."

"You don't?" My mind races. I have no idea what this guy is going on about, what he wants. He's dangerous, though, or at least it feels that way. Twenty-four hours ago I would have taken one look at this man and thought he was a nobody, just another person existing in the world.

But now he's digging around. Looking for answers, and I don't like it.

"Sure, I'll write an article about the killer when the police find him. And I'm sure he has some great trauma in his childhood that I can tap into. That's a great angle, actually." He pulls a notebook from his pocket and starts scribbling. "What kind of person would leave another person to die on the side of the road? Someone with a messed-up childhood. I bet the killer is a psychopath."

Beside me, Dave stiffens.

"Anyway," Nate says, flipping the notebook closed, "I want to know about your neighbor. What was he like? Did he have enemies? Was there anyone in particular who hated him?"

"He was fine, and no." I fiddle with my keys. "Now, if you'll excuse us, we really must be going. Good luck on your article." I gesture to his car and plaster on a smile. The Prius sounds like a spaceship whirring to life; then he backs down the driveway and is gone.

It's only when I feel like I can breathe again that I turn to Dave.

"Hey, listen," I say, grabbing his arm and squeezing it so he'll look at me. "What he said? He's wrong, okay? He's just a stupid reporter who probably has to write wedding announcements and hates it. He doesn't know anything, and he's not going to learn anything."

"Sure." Dave's still looking down the driveway.

"You're not a psychopath." I grip his arm tighter, willing him to look at me. "Dave, I'm serious. That man? He's nothing. A nobody. He doesn't know what he's talking about, and I don't want you to give him another thought, okay?"

Dave shakes his head like he's trying to focus. I can almost see the dust and cobwebs knocking loose, clearing his thoughts before he can pay attention to them. When he looks at me, he smiles. Nods.

"Alright," I say, dangling the keys between us. "Shall we? It's going to be a great day."

"A great day," Dave agrees, walking around the car to get into the passenger seat.

I watch as he gets in and buckles up. He turns and stares at me through the window. It's only when he leans over and taps on the driver's window to get my attention that I walk to the car.

A psychopath.

That's what the reporter called my son without even realizing he was doing it. I can't believe it's true, can't believe anyone could think that of Dave, but what if he's right?

No. I refuse to think that. This is my son. He's better now.

And he's going to stay that way.

16

"I just can't believe it," Carla says, gently bumping me out of the way with her hip so she can pick up a platter of food to take to customers. "Can you imagine getting run over? It's terrifying. And now his daughter is everywhere, asking questions, poking about. You know, I bet she'd find the killer herself if she didn't have to fly back out for work. I saw her yesterday at the grocery store, asking everyone what they knew. That's when she told me she had to leave town soon. It's a right shame."

"It is," I mumble, but my mind is more focused on my son. It's terrible, because if anything deserves my attention this morning, it's poor Mr. George Reece.

But trust me, he's getting more than his fair share of attention today thanks to his daughter flying into town to put pressure on the police to find his killer. His picture is on the front page of the paper, an impassioned plea from his daughter printed right underneath, begging anyone who has information about what happened to her father to come forward.

He's on the news.

He's even in the air of the diner, for goodness' sake. Every table I've helped so far has been talking about him, some in whispers, some so loud it feels like his name is reverberating in my skull.

George Reece is dead, yet I can't seem to get away from him. I barely knew him while he lived on the street, and now he's more alive than ever. It makes no sense.

"What I don't understand is how someone could hit him and then leave." Carla adjusts the platter of food balanced on her palm. She's done that twice now while watching me, like she's waiting for me to come up with some extra bit of information, a crumb to feed her, something she can survive off.

"It boggles the mind," I say, grabbing two glasses of ice water.

"No normal person would do that, would they?" She's in my way, her hip thrown out to one side to counterbalance the tray. Even though I know her stance is to stop her dropping the food, I can't help but feel like she's blocking me on purpose.

"I'm sure not," I say, then jerk my chin at her tray. "Don't you need to get a move on? Get that food out there?"

"They'll be fine." She blows a raspberry, and I try not to think about her spit landing all over the food. "They're rude, so they can wait a minute. I feel like I haven't seen you all morning."

"It's been crazy," I agree. But what I don't tell her is that I've been avoiding her the best I can. The last thing I want is for her to corner me to talk about the accident. The reporter's words still ring in my ears, and it's difficult for me to push them away.

Maybe if it had been someone else who hit our neighbor, I'd agree. That person would be a psychopath. But not my Dave. Not him. It boils my blood that anyone could insinuate that Dave is a psychopath.

"Well, maybe we can talk when the breakfast rush is over. What did you think about that reporter?"

I eyeball her. "How did you know a reporter came by the house?"

This makes her laugh. "Because he came to my place too, silly. I told him that if anyone on the street knew anything, it would be you and Dave. That you two come and go all the time, and I wouldn't be surprised if you'd seen or heard something."

"Carla." I feel my heart kick up a notch. "Why would you do that? You live closer to where he was killed, so if anyone saw anything, it would be you."

"Oh, please, Anne Marie. Like you don't know Dave is always coming and going." She levels her gaze at me. "He's up and down the road all the time when you're in bed."

A chill sashays its way up my spine, and I have to fight to keep my face straight.

"I know you two have already talked to the police," she says, speaking quickly, like she wants to cover up what she just said. "I just thought that he might have seen something. Was he home that night or out and about?"

"Home," I say, but maybe my response is too fast, too on the nose, because Carla stares at me for a moment.

"That's good." She sniffs and adjusts the tray once more. I can see how far back it's bending her wrist, but she doesn't seem to mind. Either it genuinely doesn't hurt, or she's so focused on something else that she's not paying it any attention.

Dave. She's focused on Dave.

"Sure is," I say, smiling brightly. "Anyway, I don't want my table to decide I'm not worth any tips today. I'll talk to you later, Carla."

"Of course." She moves out of my way, but I feel her gaze boring into the back of my head as I walk to my table. I give them their water and then turn, glancing over my shoulder to see if she's still watching me.

She's not. Just like a dutiful little waitress, she's bent over her table, handing out meals, her laughter loud even over the chatting crowd.

I feel like I'm in a trance as I take orders, writing them down carefully so I don't accidentally mess anything up when I pass them to the kitchen. The entire time my customers are talking to me, though, my mind is elsewhere.

On Dave.

It really feels like everyone in my life thinks horribly of my son. Benji couldn't handle him. The school doesn't know what to do with him. Even Carla, whose interactions with Dave have been minimal, thinks the worst of my son.

I stop dead in my tracks halfway back to the kitchen to put in my order. My chest feels tight, and I actually press my hand against my sternum like I'm going to be able to stop the pain in my heart.

Sweat pours down my face. I feel it gathering along my temples before it beads together, streaming down my cheeks, dripping from my chin. Heat threatens to consume me. My polyester apron suddenly weighs ten pounds, and I pluck at the strings, desperate for relief.

What if everyone is right?

Is it possible that everyone who has a problem with Dave is right? I've never considered that, never once thought about the possibility that my son could be the problem. Sure, he's a handful. And I know he takes after his father, which isn't the best thing for him.

But he's not a bad person. He's made mistakes, just like the rest of us. I'm trying so hard to be the best possible parent for him, and it's not his fault if he sometimes gets into trouble because I've failed him.

I take a deep breath, bending over and grabbing my thighs. My notepad falls to the floor as I squeeze my legs, sinking my fingers deep into the muscle.

I've failed Dave. I'm the reason he's gotten in trouble at school, the reason he has problems making and keeping friends. Everyone else is so eager to place all of the blame directly on his shoulders, but that's not fair.

It's me.

And I can't go back in time and change the way I raised Dave. I can't go back and marry someone who would be a good father, but I can make sure he's protected going forward. It's only fair. I'll protect him from the world and the people who think he's a bad person.

I owe him that.

17

MONDAY

A little more than a week passes, and George fades from news. Just like every other tragedy, whether it be a school shooting or a hurricane, something worse came along and first pushed him from the front page of the paper to page six and then right out of people's minds.

I'll admit, I'm breathing a little easier not faced with this every time I turn on the TV or open the paper. It's bad enough knowing that my son was the last person to see him alive, the last person George saw—*if he even saw the Camry coming*—but to be faced with that every single day?

It's been terrible.

Not only is George out of the papers, but I have the day off work. I stretch, rubbing my bare feet in the grass. It's a gorgeous day, with a bright blue sky and fluffy clouds. A breeze would be great, to keep the day from warming up too much. Still, I'm in the shade, avoiding the hot rays when they do peek through the clouds. Soon, though, the weather will be sweltering, and I'll be forced to spend my days off inside peering out through the windows with the AC on full blast just to stay cool.

But not today.

Today's all about me.

I yawn and reach for my book, a trashy romance Carla loaned me, when the sound of a car in the driveway makes me stiffen. My fingers are already caressing the book's cover, but I jerk them back like I've been burned and sit straight up.

The cops? That reporter?

As quickly and quietly as possible, I slip on my flip-flops, then hurry into the house, locking the back door behind me. It only takes me a minute to make my way through the front door, which I close behind me.

I've never seen the black pickup parked next to my Camry. My nerves are stretched tight as I wait as the passenger door flies open, and Dave steps out.

"Dave? Are you okay?" I leave the shade of the porch and hurry to him. "Are you sick? Why are you home early from school?"

It is early, isn't it? I risk a glance at my watch, and my heart sinks when I see it's only one o'clock.

"What are you doing here?" He crosses his arms on his chest and leans back against the truck. His face is all hard angles and planes, anger etched into his skin. "You work during the day."

"I had today off," I say, and glance at the windshield to try to make out the driver. It's too dark, too shadowed to see through, but I swear I can feel them watching. "You didn't answer my question."

He sighs. Stubs the toe of his boot into the dirt. "Jeremy

and I didn't want to spend the rest of the day in school. It's been too nice out this week to sit behind a desk."

I let what he said sink in. There's something there, something he said...wait. "How many times have you skipped school recently?"

He arches an eyebrow and laughs. Jeremy, whoever the hell that is, laughs from inside the truck. The windows are down, making it easy for him to hear everything we're saying.

My cheeks burn, but I don't look away from Dave. "How many?"

"Does it matter, Mom? Come on, don't act like you never skipped school before. Besides, it's almost the end of the year. Who cares?"

"Who cares?" My voice is going higher and higher, but I can't help it. "I care, Dave. The principal cares. Your teachers. Did you know they want to send you to the remedial high school? Is that what you want?"

He frowns. "Hell no. I'm not going there."

"Then you need to go back to class. Apologize." I'm sweating, but I can't move away from my son to step into the shade. "I'm serious, Dave. You can still fix this."

"No." Another laugh. The truck revs, like Jeremy is strongly considering gassing it and plowing right into my house.

"Dave." I lower my voice in case Jeremy has supersonic hearing even over the sound of his rumbling engine. "Come here." Without waiting for a response, I pluck Dave's sleeve and pull him away from the truck.

He groans and rolls his eyes, but walks with me.

We're under a red oak now, its sprawling branches offering some relief from the full sun. I grab my shirt and pull it away from my body, wafting it back and forth to try to cool off.

"Dave, you were being so good," I tell him, and he scoffs. Rolls his eyes.

I feel my stomach tighten.

"No, listen to me. You were. So good. We were getting along, and things were wonderful, so why would you want to ruin that? Why would you think it was a good idea to throw it all away?"

"I was good? No, Mom. I wasn't good." He shrugs, his muscles rippling. "I was scared, okay?" He leans forward, so close I can see the pockmarks on his cheeks from when he had bad acne a few years ago. "I was scared after what happened with the neighbor, but that doesn't mean I'm going to be scared forever. What, do you think I want to live my life like that?"

I frown. "No, but—"

"Did you want me to be scared forever? Not a chance, Mom. The earrings? They worked. Whoever sent those letters got scared themselves or moved away or simply decided that they had better things to do than harass me. So I'm over it."

He moves to turn back to the truck, but I grab his arm and yank him back. "You can't be *over it*," I hiss. "Murder isn't like shoplifting, Dave. It's not like jaywalking. It doesn't matter when the cops find out what happened, you can still be charged. Even if you're old and in a nursing home."

Is that true? It sounds true, but I don't know.

He sighs, the sound so heavy it feels like it came up from his toes, like he's overwhelmed by how stupid I am that he can't help himself. "Mom, you need to chill. I'm over it. You can get over it, too."

"But what if they're not done? The blackmailer? What if they come back?"

The truck engine revs again, but Dave doesn't look away from me.

"They won't. But if they do, we'll deal with them." He sucks his teeth. "Give them money, give them whatever they want. It's better than constantly living in fear, don't you think? Just accept it, Mom. This is my life."

"No," I say, but he's already jerked his arm away from me and is striding back to the truck. Jeremy yells something unintelligible from inside, and Dave laughs, then climbs in, slamming the door so hard I swear I feel it in my teeth.

Or maybe that's just because I'm gritting my jaw so tight I can already feel a headache coming on. I can't seem to move as Jeremy flies backwards down the driveway. Dave's arm rests out the window, his hand clenched into a fist. I stare at his arm, willing him to raise it in goodbye, for him to do something that will make Jeremy stop, make this afternoon change.

But he doesn't move, and Jeremy doesn't slow down, and a moment later they're out on the road, driving away, the sound of heavy bass turned up like they want me to hear them.

And I just stand in my driveway.

I thought Dave was better.

I thought we'd turned a corner, that things were going to be different, that I wasn't going to have to worry about him acting out any longer. I thought the fear of the blackmailer would be enough to keep him good, to turn him away from his wicked ways.

But I was wrong.

Slowly, like my muscles are all giving out, I sink to my

knees. Rocks dig into my bare skin, but I don't pay attention to them.

He thinks everything's going to be fine, but he's wrong. Things aren't going to be good forever, and if the blackmailer does pop back up, I don't know how we're going to deal with them. How we're going to pay them off. How I'm going to manage to scrape together the money to make them go away.

Because I can feel it in my bones. Good like this doesn't last for long, not when you don't try to preserve it. This is going to come back to bite us in the ass, I know it.

And Dave doesn't seem to care.

18

TUESDAY

I didn't expect Dave to come home for dinner last night, not after his little show of testosterone with Jeremy, so I wasn't disappointed when he didn't make his way upstairs until the wee hours of the morning. He stumbled, obviously drunk, slamming into the wall when he turned the corner to his room, and tripped over his rug.

And what did I do? I certainly didn't go to confront him. I stayed in bed, my face growing hot, frustration coursing through my body as I listened to him kick his shoes off into the wall and fall into bed with a groan.

Now I'm at the table, on my second cup of coffee already. I have a later start time in the mornings so I can make sure Dave gets to school on time. At first, when Dave got a little older, I asked him to take the bus to school in the mornings. It seemed like a great idea, a way for him to get going on his day and me to start mine without the two of us requiring each other, but it only worked for a week or so.

Then he started skipping. Even as a little kid he would refuse to get on the bus. He'd run into the woods and hide, waiting there until he knew nobody would be looking for him; then he'd hurry back to the house and let himself in with the key I left under the fake rock in the garden.

That was back when I had enough energy to try to grow a garden here. I planted so many flowers and even a few vegetables that first summer, but the weeds quickly took over, choking everything out, and I couldn't bear the thought of getting on my knees to weed when everything in my life seemed to be spiraling out of control.

Part of me wants to punish Dave by letting him stay in bed to sleep off his hangover. The terrible part of me relishes the thought of my son aching, his mouth dry and parched, his eyeballs pounding with every heartbeat. But letting him ignore the consequences of his actions is not what a good mother does, and I'm certainly not going to allow him to skip school because he made this terrible decision.

No, he needs to get up. Face what he's done.

Right as I'm about to hurry upstairs to wake him, my phone rings. I fumble it from the table and almost swipe the screen on, but then I pause. Look at the caller ID.

The high school. There's only one reason why they'd be calling me this early in the morning, and I'm not interested in hearing from the principal about how terrible Dave is. I have no desire to let her screech into my ear about kicking him out of school.

So I silence it, joy shooting through me as I mash the button on the side of the phone. Then I put it back down on the table and hurry up the stairs.

In the hall outside Dave's room, I pause. His door is cracked, but he didn't seem to hear me moving around this morning as I got ready for my day. He's passed out and only been in bed for a few hours, but I have to remind myself that

that's not my fault. Dave made that choice last night when he went out drinking, and now he has to live with it.

Girding myself against how angry he's going to be, I push open his door. It's dark in here, a cave, and cool, but it smells like stale beer and whiskey. I wrinkle my nose and cross the room to his bed.

"Dave." When I touch his shoulder, he doesn't move. I swear, he looks like he could be dead. His head is at a strange angle, his mouth is slack, his lips dry. I grab his shoulder, giving him a little shake. "Dave, wake up."

Nothing. No jerking awake, no swearing at me for interrupting his sleep, nothing.

Falling to my knees, I put my hand on his chest and stare at the spot, willing it to rise and fall. It's difficult to see anything clearly in this dim light, but I don't look away until I see it—a tiny movement, just enough to make me exhale hard.

As soon as the relief hits me, it's replaced by something else. Something I've never felt towards my son before. I've loved him since the moment I found out I was pregnant. I've worried for him, hoped for him. I've cried over him and begged him to be better. I've been frustrated and hurt, hopeful and anxious.

But never angry.

It feels like I'm not in control of my body as I march across his bedroom and flick on the light. The groan that comes from the bed shouldn't make me smile, but it does.

"Wake up," I call, making my voice a singsong, which I know he hates. "It's time to get up and go to school, Dave. You don't want to be late."

Are those my hands reaching for him? I see them grab his blankets, watch as they rip them off and to the side.

Dave's still wearing his clothes from last night, and he rolls over, throwing his hand over his face to block out the light.

"Don't hide from me," I tell him, grabbing his arm and pulling it back down. Normally he could fight me. There's usually no way I can force my son to do anything physical he doesn't want to, but he doesn't resist now. His arm is a hunk of meat, nothing more, and it falls over the side of the bed when I let go.

"Please, no."

The words are such a surprise that I pause for a moment, considering what I'm doing, but then I walk to his stereo and click it on.

Normally I hate the loud music he has pumping in his room. I hate the way it feels like there are a dozen tiny men in my head, all of them with hammers, all of them pounding on my skull in a bid to escape.

Angry chords fill the room, and Dave groans again.

"I'm not telling you again," I say, walking over to look down on him. "You need to get up, Dave. You don't want to miss school."

This anger I feel threatens to overtake me. I know I need to calm down, need to somehow take a deep breath so I can handle this like an adult because there's no way Dave will be able to do that, but I can't stop myself.

I want him up.

I want him to behave.

I want the scared Dave back, as terrible as that sounds.

"I'm taking you to school in half an hour," I tell him, my hands on my hips, my teeth gritted together. "I don't care that you're hungover. I don't care that you and Jeremy apparently make the worst decisions when you're together. You can't be a sloppy teenager any longer, do you understand me? Your life changed. *You* changed your life."

He still has his eyes obstinately squeezed shut and is refusing to look at me, but that's fine. I'm going to get through to my son no matter what I have to do.

"Half an hour," I tell him. "If you're not up, dressed, and standing in front of me ready to go to school, I'm going to do something drastic."

"Yeah, like what?" His eyes still aren't open, but he manages to speak from the corner of his mouth.

That I don't know. But there is one thing I know, and it's this—I've had a taste of Dave being good. It was wonderful.

I can't go back to this.

19

My phone hasn't stopped ringing since I dropped Dave off at school. Well, that's an exaggeration. It rings; I ignore it. Ten minutes later it rings again, and I turn off the sound. The phone calls were even five minutes apart at one point, if you can believe that.

Fear eats at the back of my mind, but I push it away and instead focus on work. That's the best thing for me to do right now, since it's not like I have to worry about who's calling me.

It's the school. Principal Byler, to be exact, probably blowing up my phone in a desperate attempt to get me to come back to the high school so we can chat. So she can make me feel bad about Dave. So she can tell me I need to come get him and take him home, but it's not going to happen.

She has a responsibility to educate him. I know how this works. My job was to get him to school, and I did that. What she does with him now is up to her, and it's definitely not something I can worry about, not when I'm currently carrying six entrees out to a table of middle-aged women with matching haircuts.

Long in front, short in back. Highlights. Chunky ones. I knew from the moment they walked in that they'd be trouble.

They all have dark circles under their eyes. The one closest to me doesn't even acknowledge my presence when I put the plate down in front of her. She makes a grunting sound, like a pig, then stabs her French toast like it wronged her in middle school.

"Is there anything else I can get you?" My voice is shockingly chipper, all things considered.

"Are you sure you don't have any champagne in the back?" It's the only woman who looks like she doesn't completely hate her life. They're struggling, and I could use a mimosa just to deal with them.

"No alcohol," I say brightly. "You'll have to wait for a bar to open to be able to get anything to drink. Do you want me to make you ladies a fresh pot of coffee?"

She shakes her head. The rest of them stare down at their plates, obviously overwhelmed by the food in front of them.

I feel a smile play on the corners of my mouth. It's terrible to rejoice in someone else's pain, and I know that. But it's honestly just nice for someone else to be having a worse morning than I am.

"Just let me know if you need anything, or feel free to flag me down." I grin at each of them, waiting until the one closest to me, the one who really looks green around the gills, looks up at me. "I'll be back later to check on you."

The grin slides off my face as soon as I turn around.

Richard and Carla are talking to someone, and even though I can't see the guy's face, my stomach sinks.

Why, though? It's entirely possible it's just a customer who wanted a little extra attention from Richard. Maybe someone got lost, and they swung into Early Bird to get directions.

Not everything going on is about me.

My movements feel robotic, my joints stiff, as I walk back to the kitchen. To get there and check on the food for another one of my tables, I have to walk right by the trio. Richard's voice is low and grumbly, like he's upset about something, and I hold my breath so I can hear him.

"Are you sure you saw someone steal a car from our back parking lot? You don't think it was just the driver and they had trouble opening their door?"

The man shifts position, and I freeze, turning to look at the three of them. Richard will freak out if he realizes I'm standing here watching and listening, but I can't help myself. I'm dying to know what exactly is going on.

"Oh, I don't think it was his car." The man's voice is high-pitched, but not shaky. He might be worried or uncomfortable facing off against Richard, but you'd never know it. "He broke out the passenger window to let himself in."

My stomach sinks. It feels like my blood has turned to sludge, and I walk over to the three of them without realizing I'm moving.

"Okay, I'll have to call the police." Richard throws up his hands like this is the worst thing in the world to have happened. Literal aliens could come blasting out of the sky and he wouldn't be as bothered as he is about calling the police.

"Can you stick around and talk to the cops?" That's

Carla, her voice syrupy-sweet. She's laying it on thick, and I can see why. The man is attractive, with a strong jaw and short black hair.

"I really can't," he says, and her shoulders slump a little. "I'm sorry, I have to get to work. But I can leave you a description of the car and the man I saw breaking into it."

No. I don't want him to tell her anything else. Even without him saying another word, I feel like I know what he's going to say.

"The man was tall," he begins.

I close my eyes, feeling my cheeks already start to flame.

"I think it was a teenager, now that I think about it, but he was big. Really big." He holds his hand above his head a few inches to indicate how tall the guy was.

How tall *Dave* was.

"And big hands. No beard. Brown hair." The man shrugs. "Hoodie and jeans. Nothing really special, nothing that would make him stand out. Just a guy breaking a window."

"On a Camry?" I can't stop from inserting myself into the conversation. "Was it an old black Camry?"

The guy nods. "Hey, how did you—"

"Don't call the police." I turn to Richard, who's staring at me like he's never seen me before. "Please, Richard, I'm begging you. Let me handle this."

He frowns. "Let me guess: Dave?"

I'm not just blushing right now, I feel like I'm completely on fire. Every cell of my being is burning, and it's partly because Carla, Richard, and this other guy are all staring at me.

"Dave," I whisper, nodding. "Please let me handle it. I promise you I can get this under control. But if you call the police and they get involved, then there really isn't any coming back from this. I can help him. I can get through to him. Don't get the police involved."

"Anne Marie." Richard has completely forgotten about anyone else in the room. It feels like it's just the two of us, like everything else has fallen away. It's unnerving.

"Richard, he's my son."

"He's a nuisance."

I shake my head, ready to argue my point until I'm blue in the face, but Richard cuts me off.

"If you walk out of here to handle something because your son is out of control, then don't bother coming back."

"What?" Surely I didn't hear him correctly. I stare at him, then my eyes flick over to Carla. Judging by the shocked expression on her face, I'd say I heard him perfectly.

"If you leave Early Bird before the scheduled end of your shift, then I will fire you. You won't ever be allowed back, Anne Marie. I've told you and told you that you need to keep the drama with your son out of work, yet you continue to allow it to infest your day-to-day job."

"Richard, he's in trouble."

"He's not *in* trouble, Anne Marie. He *is* trouble. There's a distinction, and until you figure it out, until you learn your lesson and stop letting him control every single aspect of your life, you're never going to go anywhere. You'll be working in a diner just like this one for the rest of your life, always making excuses for your son, a grown man who should know better."

The man who saw Dave break my window slowly backs up. His eyes are wide, and he looks shocked. He glances at Richard, then at me, then back to Richard before finally speaking. "So you have it under control?" He sounds meek.

"It's fine," I say, through gritted teeth. "Thank you for letting us know what was going on."

The man nods, then backs up before turning and practically fleeing for the door.

I watch him out of the corner of my eye, but I don't look away from Richard, not when the two of us need to finish this.

"What's it going to be, Anne Marie? Will you stay at work and let your son finally figure out what happens when he keeps messing up, or are you going to rush out to save the day yet again?" Richard doesn't sound angry. He sounds resigned. Tired. Like a father who has just had it with his child's antics, a father who knows better than his kid about how terrible life can get if you're not careful.

"Anne Marie," Carla says, stepping closer to me, "you can't lose this job."

I know that.

"I'll stay," I finally say, and the words feel like I've given up, like I'm making a huge mistake, but what other option do I have? I don't know where Dave is. I can call him, but when he gets in a mood like this, he usually refuses to answer his phone.

And even if I were to walk out of here right now, where would I go? I don't have a car, Dave made sure of that. I'm stuck here, stuck in this dead-end job I can't escape, stuck with a son whom I love more than anything but who keeps messing up.

I thought we'd turned a corner, I really had.

"Get to work, then," Richard tells me. "You have customers." He gives me a nod, then walks away, leaving me standing with Carla.

"Hey, I'll get you home after work, okay? Dave will show back up." Her fingers flutter against my shoulder.

"He was being so good," I tell her, desperate for someone to understand that things were different. Were better. "Carla, he was being so good, and then this."

"What are you going to do?"

I can't answer.

I don't know.

20

Carla drives me home in her cherry red Jeep, running her mouth a mile a minute about the various customers we had in today, but I'm barely listening. My face is turned to the window, my forehead resting against the glass. It's cool in the Jeep, with the AC blowing right on me, but I still feel sweaty and hot, like I've just run a marathon.

"Hello, are you in there?" Carla takes her right hand off the wheel long enough to reach over and tap me on the side of the head. I whip around to look at her, anger creasing my brow, but she just laughs. "It's going to be fine, Anne Marie. You just have to relax. Seriously. You're more tightly wound than a nun." She grins, then looks back at the road.

We're almost at the exact location where George Reece was hit. I know it's silly, because I don't believe in ghosts, but I can't help but think I feel a chill race up my arms every time I drive past where he died.

"I'm fine, Carla. It's just been a really long day, but you know that. You were there for it."

"Sure was. What I don't understand, though, is why that boy of yours doesn't settle down. He's a handful, isn't he?"

Instead of answering, I check my phone. I've called him a dozen times and sent more than twice that many text messages, but it's like Dave fell off the face of the planet. He's out of control. I know that. Everyone else knows that. The problem is, I don't know what to do about it.

"Anne Marie, what are you going to do about Dave?" Now Carla lightly touches my knee in a bid to get my attention.

"I'll talk to him," I say, turning to face her with a nod. "He's not completely gone, Carla. He just hasn't had the easiest life so far."

"And you have?" She slows through the turn onto our road. "Anne Marie, you've been a single mom the entire time you've had that boy, haven't you?"

I nod.

"And has he ever had anything resembling a father figure?"

"I had a boyfriend," I find myself saying, although I'm not sure why I'm spilling my guts to Carla. It's not like I know her very well, but it just feels good to talk to someone. *Anyone.* "But he just ended things with me."

She tsks. "Because of Dave?"

I can't answer that, but I don't need to. She's not stupid. She can figure out what I'm saying without me saying anything.

"Sometimes, Anne Marie, love isn't enough." She navigates the turns on the road carefully before slowing down to pull into my driveway. "I know you love him. Dave."

"More than anything." I'm suddenly overwhelmed with the urge to make sure she understands just how strongly I feel for my son. Not like there should be any question, not when I'm willing to do whatever it takes to keep him happy, keep him healthy, keep him out of trouble.

Because he should be in trouble, shouldn't he? Because of Mr. George—

She pulls to a stop right where I always park the Camry. Even as we pulled into the driveway, I felt this stupid, sudden hope that Dave would be here, that he'd be lounging on the front porch, that my car would be parked on the grass where he always leaves it.

So to have it not here feels like a blow to the gut.

"You're a good momma, Anne Marie. You can't blame yourself that Dave's got problems. Sometimes kids just do." She presses her lips together and looks past me to the house.

"They do, but Dave's really growing up," I tell her, desperate for her to see some good in my son. "We've been having a lot of fun together."

"That's good, Anne Marie. That's real good." Her voice is sad, and she looks away from the house to focus on me. "Call me in the morning if you need a ride to work. I'm not coming in until later, but I'm happy to swing by your place and pick you up."

"I'll have the car back," I say, doing my best to sound more confident than I feel. "Thanks, but I don't think you need to worry about me." The car door is locked, and I fumble with the handle before finally getting it open and stepping out into the heat. "Thank you, though. And thanks for the ride home."

"Not a problem." She flaps her hand at me like she's waving away my words. "Call me. I'll help you, Anne Marie. You need it."

Her words ring in my ears as I slam the door and walk up

to my porch. Behind me, I hear her making a thousand-point-turn, which is annoying, but probably the safest way to get out of our driveway without getting hit. I wait at the front door until I hear her pull out on her way to her house, then slowly turn and sink down into a porch chair.

I always smell like the diner after a shift. A little sweaty, a little like coffee, a little like grease. It's gross, and normally I want to change as quickly as possible. Rinse it all out of my hair. Pull on some jeans and a shirt that will make me feel like a human again.

But right now all I want is my son. After turning my phone over and over in my hand, I finally call him again.

It rings three times; then he must send me to voicemail because the message picks up.

You've reached Dave. You know what to do. If you don't, you can go to—

I hang up. He'll come home. He has to. I'll talk to him, help him get his head on straight.

And then we'll work this out.

Resigned, I stand and stretch, then head inside. Just as I put my hand on the doorknob, though, I hear a crash.

Someone's in my house.

21

I freeze. For a moment I imagine Carla pulling back into the driveway, leaning out the window, calling to me to get in her car, that she knows where Dave is, that she'll take me there. My ears hurt from straining for any sound, but I don't have to listen hard for what comes next.

There's another loud crash. Then, "Shit!"

I step back from the door, dropping my hand from the handle. Someone's in the kitchen, someone loud and unafraid of being heard, and I don't know who it is.

Dave? It could be Dave, maybe, although that didn't sound like his voice. He swears all the time, but *shit* is pretty low on his list of words to use when he's upset. Besides, if he's here, then where's my Camry?

The thought of calling the police flits through my mind, but I push it away as quickly as I think it. It was terrifying enough to have them show up on my porch after George died. The last thing I want is to willingly invite them here. Not that I think there are any clues around that prove Dave killed George.

But what if there are?

My heart is still pounding in my chest, but I steel myself and press my ear up against the kitchen door. Someone's making a hell of a lot of noise in there. Gripping my purse, I pull it closer to my chest.

It could be the blackmailer.

What if Dave got another note and I don't know about it? What if there was something else the person wanted, something more than my earrings, and when Dave didn't deliver, they decided to come here and look for it themselves? It's possible, I guess, although what could they want from me? My earrings were the only things I had that were worth anything at all. And now they're gone.

Anger and sadness battle in me, and I close my eyes.

Call the police? Open the door and start screaming? Run to Carla's?

There's no good option here, but if someone is in my house because Dave's in trouble, then I want to help him out. I *have* to help him out. I grip the doorknob, ignoring the slick of sweat that makes it slippery, then count down from ten.

On *one*, I turn the knob. Throw the door open. It slams hard into the wall, ricocheting back at me, but I block it with my palm as I rush into the house, my purse swinging free and whacking into my side with every step.

"Stop right there!" I scream the words, unsure of what else to do. *It was really stupid not to call the cops, Anne Marie.*

A man kneels by the sink, his torso hidden inside the cupboard. As I watch, he stiffens, slowly leaning back to crawl out from where he was—what? What could he possibly have been doing or looking for under the sink?

In a moment of brilliance I shove my hand into my purse. "I have a gun!" My fingers close around the pack of

Tic Tacs I've had rattling around in the bottom of my purse for the past month or so.

"Hey, I don't want any trouble," the man says, slowly turning, then unfolding himself to his full height. "Don't shoot." He holds his hands up, and it's just now that I realize how young he really is.

He's not a man. Not technically, anyway. Not any more than Dave is a man. It's unnerving, seeing him in my kitchen, though. It doesn't matter how old or young he is, I don't like the fact that he's here, in my space, without my permission.

"Who are you?" My voice only shakes a little, and I'm prouder of that fact than I probably should be.

"I'm a friend of Dave's."

Sweat trickles down my back when I hear his words. It's not that I don't believe him, but why the hell would my son send someone to the house like this? Unless he's lying. He could be lying.

I take a step back and jerk my chin towards the front door. "Outside. Now. And go slow or I'll shoot you."

He keeps his hands up and slowly inches around the kitchen, not taking his eyes off me as we reach the door. I left it open, and he backs through it, feeling behind him before stepping back.

Thank goodness there's a breeze out here. It helps to cool me off, dry some of the sweat on my face. I exhale hard and eyeball the boy. "Now. Who are you?"

He pauses, scuffs his toe into the porch like he's not going to answer me.

"I have a gun. I'm also happy to call the cops. Or you can tell me who you are, and we can get through this together."

"Jeremy." The boy's eyes flash up to my face.

"Jeremy with the big truck?" When he nods, I continue, "Where is that truck?"

"I parked it around a bend in your road. I didn't want anyone to know I was here."

That tracks. I never saw the guy's face when Dave was here with him before, but I have no doubt in my mind that any one of my son's friends would be perfectly willing to rob him and me blind if they got the chance. Why Dave can't have normal, good, reliable friends, I don't know.

"What were you looking for?" I'm squeezing the little box of Tic Tacs so hard the plastic corners are digging into my skin, but I don't release it. It feels like holding on to it as tightly as possible is the only thing keeping me from losing my mind. And if I move my hand, he might think I'm going to shoot him. When I don't produce a gun, he'll know I'm full of it.

"Drugs." His jaw tightens.

"Under my kitchen sink? Try again."

His shoulders seem to soften, and he gives his head a little shake. "Money. Dave owes me money. I know he doesn't have any, but I thought you might have some stashed away. I just wanted to get it and go, I promise. I wasn't going to do anything else."

"What does he owe you money for?" I already know the answer, or at least I think I do, so why am I asking?

"Drugs." This time when he says the word, he doesn't look like he's lying. He was staring at a spot right over my shoulder, but now he's looking at me. "He owes me for buying them for him. I was just coming to collect because he won't pay up."

"Weed? Or something else?"

"Just weed."

That doesn't explain why he's been so volatile recently. If anything, I'd think that smoking a little pot would calm him down. Chill him out. But it's not worth digging deeper into this guy's lie.

"How much money?"

"One hundred." Again his jaw tightens.

"Be honest."

He shakes his head. "You're a pain in the ass, you know that? Fifty."

"I've heard it all before," I tell him. "I'm going to get you the cash, but you don't move or I will change my mind and shoot, do you understand?" When he nods, I let go of the Tic Tac box and pull out my wallet. I don't have a lot of money and never really carry cash around with me, but I have tips from today and the money I put aside to go to the grocery store later. It physically hurts to pull out two twenties and a ten, but I do it and toss them on the ground between us before slipping my wallet back in my purse and grabbing the Tic Tac box again.

He stares at the money. His hands are still up in the air, but he doesn't move.

"Don't give Dave drugs again," I tell him. "Don't sell them to him; don't take him to buy them. If I ever see your face on my property again, I will call the cops and tell them you attacked me." I pause to let that sink in. "Is that clear?"

"Crystal."

"Good." I take a few steps back so I can easily get in my house. "I'm going inside. Once I shut the door, you can get the money, and then you're gone. Never again, Jeremy. Don't come back here."

"Okay." He licks his lower lip. I stare at him for a minute, trying to decide if there's a better option here, but I really don't think there is. I need him gone, not just from my driveway, but from Dave's life.

If only there were a way to permanently remove him—but I stop that thought before it can run away from me.

"And if you tell Dave what happened, I'll find out. I'll call the police. My son is dead to you."

He nods.

I step backwards into the house, my heart pounding in my chest. For a moment, we lock eyes; then I slam the door shut and throw the bolt before hurrying to the kitchen window. He's already grabbing the cash and stuffing it into his pocket while looking around him, then takes off down the driveway.

I sink to the floor and rest my head on my knees. My heart's beating so hard I feel like I'm going to throw up, so I force myself to take deep, slow breaths. After a minute, I feel less dizzy, and I grab my phone to call Dave. There's no answer, so I finally do leave a message.

"Dave, it's your mother. I need to talk to you. You can't keep ignoring my calls and running around town like this. It isn't sustainable." I pause, considering what to say next. I could threaten him, just like I threatened Jeremy, but Dave would see through it in a heartbeat. He knows I wouldn't ever do anything to hurt him.

"Come home," I say, because what else is there to do?

I need him home so I can fix this. So I can protect him.

22

I'm in my pajamas and almost ready for bed when Dave finally stumbles in through the front door. I heard my car in the driveway but couldn't get up, couldn't force myself to look out the window to see my son driving it, so the first look I get of him is when he spots me in the living room, a blanket pulled up to my chest, a cool cup of chamomile on the side table next to me.

"You're home late," I say, doing my best to keep my voice calm. "Did you have a good day?"

He grunts, leans against the doorframe.

Yesterday was a nightmare. Today was no better. It's like those few days of Dave being so good, so kind and thoughtful, never happened. They were a fever dream, just something I wanted so badly I almost wished it into existence, and now I have to wake up and live in the real world, no matter how painful that really is.

"I needed your car." He stares at me like he's waiting for me to argue with him, but in all the years of being his mother, I've learned not to do that. You have to let him talk his way through things, or into things, so I just sit quietly.

"I needed it." He rubs his hands together and watches me.

"Fine. Next time, though, ask for the keys. I had to catch a ride home with Carla. You stranded me, Dave. And now I have to figure out how to pay for the window. I had to keep someone from calling the police on you. And you just...don't seem to care about any of that."

"What do you want me to say, Mom? Sorry? I shouldn't have done that? I won't do it again?"

"Any of that would be nice," I say, "but I'm not going to hold my breath." I stand up, letting the blanket puddle into the chair behind me. "How about this, Dave? Someone knows what you did, so maybe you should consider not showing your ass around town? I had to keep someone at the diner from calling the cops because he saw you breaking out the window of my car. What then? What if they somehow found out what else you did?"

"Then I'd wonder why you told them, since you're the only person who knows the truth." He glares at me, his nostrils flaring as he sucks in huge breaths.

"But I'm not, am I?" My voice, in comparison, is quieter.

He leans forward to listen to me.

"There's someone else who knows what you did, and don't you forget that, Dave. Someone else is well aware that you're a murderer, and unless you want the cops sniffing around, you should probably stop doing things like stealing cars."

The tension between us grows. It's almost palpable, like it's an entity in the room. I want to look away from him so I don't have to see the anger etched on his face, but I'm afraid to break eye contact. As soon as one of us does that, the spell will be over, and he'll leave here. We won't ever talk about this again, I'm sure of it.

Not because I'm scared of him. I'm not. I just don't want to lose him. And Dave's the kind of guy to pull back from people when they stand up to him, when they don't do what he wants.

"It was an emergency."

"Drugs?" I offer, still keeping my voice light.

"A girl," he says.

"So you skipped school to take a girl...where? And does the principal not know, because she's normally blowing up my phone by now telling me that she's going to kick you out of school even though she can't. Apparently. Somehow." I'm rambling, and he's just staring at me, a small smile curling up the corner of his mouth. "What, Dave?"

"She kicked me out." He crams his hand into his pocket and pulls out a piece of paper. It's folded and crumpled, and I have to take a moment to smooth it out after he presses it into my hand. "I'm out of school. Gone. Donezo."

"No." My hand shakes as I read the paper, and I hate that I can't stop it, but this is insane. Impossible. "She told me she couldn't kick you out. That the alternative high school didn't have room for you, and since I can't homeschool you, she didn't have a choice. She had to keep you as a student."

"Looks like a slot at the alternative school came open." Dave yawns, stretching his hands high above his head. "You think they keep attendance there? Ooh, Mom, maybe I won't be the worst kid at the school, what do you think about that? You're so used to me being the bad one, but maybe I'll be a good one now. That would be nice."

"Dave, this says I have to come to school tomorrow and

finish the paperwork." I look up at him, my heart sinking. "I'm working tomorrow. There's no way I can get off work. Richard will fire me."

"Then I guess I'm not going to school." He grins and shrugs, the movements languid and easy, like he doesn't have a care in the world. Like he didn't just drop this bombshell in my lap without any concern for how I'm going to take care of it.

"No. Dave, no." Panic flutters through me, and I drop the paper to the ground as I dive for my phone. It's where I left it, right by my tea, and my fingers fumble to turn it on. "I'm going to call Mrs. Byler. I'll talk to her and get this straightened out. She told me you wouldn't be kicked out of school. She pretty much promised me! She can't go back on that now."

My vision is blurred, and I angrily wipe my hand across my eyes to wipe away the tears. Everything about this day has sucked. I've been doing everything in my power to protect my son, and it feels like he's thwarting me at every turn, like he just doesn't care what happens to him.

"Mom, no." Dave grabs the phone from me, holding it above his head when I jump for it. "You can't call her! It's eleven at night. And what are you going to say that you haven't already said? Just let it go. It's not worth it. I don't care, and you shouldn't, either."

"What do you mean by *it's not worth it*?" I hiss the words at him. "You're my son; of course you're worth it. But if I take tomorrow off, I lose my job. How can I keep everything together when you're so hell-bent on tearing it all apart?"

"Call in sick. Tell Richard you have the flu."

"I need money. For groceries." For a moment, telling him about Jeremy crosses my mind, but I push the thought away.

That's my little secret. Dave would hate how I handled it. And he would still try to be friends with Jeremy. I can't let that happen.

"You worked today. Use today's tips." He sighs. "I'm sorry, Mom. I know you want more from me, but I just can't do it."

"But you could. You were so good recently, Dave."

"I was scared. There's a difference." He hands me back my phone. "And scared is no way to live your life. Good night, Mom."

He leaves me standing in the living room, my head spinning. Every time I try to fix things, they end up getting more messed up. But something has to change, right? Dealing with Jeremy today was just the start.

23

WEDNESDAY

Dave watches as I pour myself a cup of coffee. I know he wants to know my plans for the day, what I'm going to do, but I haven't decided. Call in sick and miss out on making the money we need to pay for groceries, so I can try to work things out with his school? Or go to work and throw him to the wolves for what is possibly the first time in his life?

I'm so torn.

"Hey, get the paper, would you?" I turn to Dave, doing my best not to look him in the eyes. He'll be able to tell that I'm confused about what to do if we make eye contact. The last thing I want is to have to deal with him pressuring me one way or the other. I tossed and turned all night, trying to decide what to do, and now I feel like I was hit by a semi.

Not the joke to make.

"Sure." He's been leaning against the counter but pushes off it to walk over to the front door. "You know, Mom, I don't have to go back to school. If they don't want me there, then I don't want to be there."

The spatula I'm using to poke at scrambled eggs drips onto the floor, but I ignore it. "And what, Dave? You don't go to school, and you're going to...what? Get a job?"

He scoffs.

"I didn't think so. You can't just hang out all the time with your friends. You can't possibly think that would be an acceptable thing for you to do. Geez, Dave, use your brain. You have to go back to school. It's the only way you're going to have a better life than you do now."

"Did you finish high school?" He shoots the words at me like they have barbs, like he doesn't already know the answer to that one.

"You know I didn't," I say, my voice even and measured. I'm doing my best to stay calm, but it's hard. "I wish I did, though. Things would be different."

Maybe if I hadn't gotten knocked up by an abusive guy when I was in high school, I would have graduated. My parents wouldn't have cut me out of their lives. I would have found a real job, or maybe gone to college. There's nothing wrong with working a trade, but I could have gone on, gotten a college degree.

But I didn't. And I want more for Dave, want it desperately for him. What drives me nuts is that he doesn't seem too worried about wanting it for himself. He's only focused on the now, what he can get now, what he can get away with, and he has no idea how important it is to focus on the future, to try to better yourself.

"Yeah, so different. Maybe none of this would have happened." He's angry, and he spits the words at me, but finally opens the front door and walks out onto the porch.

Just having him gone from the room is a relief, and I sigh,

sagging against the counter, not even caring that the eggs are going to burn.

"Just the paper," I call, when he hasn't come right back. "Don't go wandering off, Dave. I want to read what's going on in the world."

Silence.

"Dave." Closing my eyes, I take a deep breath. Why is it that he thinks he always has to push my buttons? While it would be so easy for him to go out there and bring back the paper, he has to lallygag, has to get sucked into something else that takes his attention, has to find something to do without telling me he's going to disappear for a moment.

This. This is the problem. I snap the burner off and drop my spatula on the counter. I deal with so much from Dave, but one of the things that really pushes my buttons is how he never takes my feelings into consideration. I wanted to read the paper while drinking my coffee and having a bite of breakfast, but if he's going to drag his feet about bringing it in, then I'm not going to have time.

I know I'm just trying to avoid making a decision about what I'm going to do today, but I don't care. I just need that paper. Then I can read it. I can get my morning back on track. For a few minutes I can avoid thinking about what my son has done and how I have to pick up the pieces.

"Dave, I just want the paper," I say, heaving a sigh as I walk across the kitchen. He even left the front door open, and already there's a moth inside, fluttering uselessly against the kitchen light. I hear its wings bat against the fixture but don't slow down to help it.

I can't even help myself. Help my son. How in the world can I help anything else?

"Dave." My voice has a sharp edge to it, but I can't help it.

"Honestly, Dave, how hard is it to come out here and get the paper? It's a simple thing, but you won't do it. Why won't you just help me?"

I hate the desperation in my voice, hate how useless I feel when Dave's like this, when he won't listen, when he won't help me out, and I have to do it all myself. It's exhausting. And yet, I don't have a choice.

Finally, I'm outside. The ring of trees surrounding our house means we never get to see a gorgeous sunrise. We have to wait until the fingers of dawn have clawed their way high enough up into the sky to be visible, so right now everything off the porch, away from the light, is shrouded in dark.

I can't even see my car, that's how thick the dark is. Half an hour and things will have lightened up enough to easily walk around, to see the world in shades of gray, but right now Dave and I are in a circle of light, the dull overhead light the only thing holding back the dark.

"Paper," I say, grabbing it from the porch where he left it. "Come on, Dave. I just wanted the paper." This is turning into a bigger deal than it should, but that's only because I've been holding it all in. I've refused to blow up at him, to show him how upset I really am, to allow my emotions to get the best of me, and now they're seeping out, like water through cracks in a dam.

"Mom." His voice has a quiver to it, something I don't hear often, and I freeze in the process of unfolding the paper, my hands clenching tight to grip it. "Look at this."

I don't want to.

I think I noticed he was holding something when I came out here. If I'm honest with myself, I saw the piece of paper in his hand, and somewhere in my subconscious, I knew what it was, knew it was going to be something we had to deal with even though I didn't want to.

"Mom," he says, his voice strangled. "Please."

No.

I want to go inside. Read the paper. Drink my coffee. I want to go to work and take him to school and not have to worry about what he's done and who knows the truth and what they're going to do about it.

"Please."

I turn. I'm still gripping the newspaper tightly enough to crumple it, even to rip it, so I can't reach out and take the piece of paper from him, but I don't need to.

It's another note. From the blackmailer.

24

The chill of the wood porch cuts through my jeans, but I can't move. I had to sit down, or my legs were going to do it for me. I'd slowly lowered myself to the porch, but my eyes never left the paper in Dave's hand. I can't stop staring at it.

"Tell me what it says." It's the first time I've spoken since Dave called out to me, and my voice sounds rusty and unused, or maybe that's just the pounding in my ears.

Dave clears his throat. He glances at me, then back at the paper in his hand before slowly sitting next to me. "They want two thousand dollars."

"No." It's a whisper, but Dave hears it.

"Mom, we—"

"Don't have that kind of money," I finish for him. "I don't know what to tell you, and I wish there were something else to say, but it's paycheck to paycheck over here."

His jaw tightens, and I hurry to smooth it over, to make what I just said less painful.

"It's hard, Dave, but it's not your fault. Not anyone's fault.

It's just that life is so expensive, and I'm trying, I really am, but I can't do it all. I've tried to do it all for years now, and we're hanging in there, but there's no cushion like that."

"But that's what they want." He sounds like a little kid who's convinced that, through arguing, he'll be able to change the outcome, bend it to his will. And I wish he could.

I shake my head. "I have half of that. That's it. And that means no buying anything until I get back to work and get more tips. That means I can't exactly take today off. No calling in sick."

He opens his hand, and the paper flutters to the porch next to me. Without really thinking, I pick it up. I'm not sure what I expect, but maybe he was joking. Lying. Maybe, for some reason, he thought it would be funny to tell me that it was blackmail even though it really wasn't.

But the words stare up at me. The same handwriting as before. The message is clear and just what he said.

"But they'll call the police if we don't get them the money." Dave sits down next to me.

"Do you have money?" It's a Hail Mary, and I know it, but Dave doesn't have a job; he doesn't—

"I have some."

"How?"

He stares at me. "Do you really want to know?"

"No." I swallow. "Do you have a thousand?"

"Maybe." His voice is hard. "I might. Let me see that." He takes the note from me. "Two thousand. In the park. This weekend. What do we do?"

"We take them the money," I say automatically. "That, or you get turned in to the police."

"They'd get in trouble, too, for blackmail."

I shake my head. "I'm pretty sure murder trumps blackmail anytime, Dave. Are you willing to go to jail just to get them in trouble, too?"

"Do you think they'll stop?" He sounds scared. A little kid turning to his mother in the hope that she can fix the mess he made. But I don't think this is a mess I can fix. Not easily, not permanently.

"I think we have to try," I say, reaching out to touch his knee. "I think that if we ignore this note, they'll go to the cops, and then we won't have any move. Ignoring it sounds like a good idea until you realize that they have all the cards."

"So I just, what? Give them all of my hard-earned money?"

I stare at him. "*Our* hard-earned money, Dave. And yes, unless you have a better idea."

He falls silent, and I stare out into the yard. I know the car is out there, the driveway. I know there's a bit of scrubby grass and then the thick trees, but I can't see any of it right now. Maybe I'd feel better if I could, if we weren't surrounded by dark. Some light would be nice.

"We could take care of the problem."

"That's what we're doing," I say, sighing. "The only way to take care of this problem is to just pay the money. Deal with it that way, and hope they don't come back. There's nothing else to do in this situation, Dave, unless you want to go to prison. And guess what? I'd be going too, for trying to protect you." A lump forms in my throat.

"No, not pay them." He turns to me, grabbing my hand.

The contact is so sudden and unexpected that I almost jerk my hand away, but he's squeezing my fingers, gripping them so tightly I can't move.

"*Take care* of them."

"I heard you," I say, "but I don't get it."

And then I do. It's not just the words he repeated, but the way he said them, each one loaded with meaning and promise. It's how he squeezed my fingers tighter, how he stared me right in the eyes like he was terrified I was going to look away from him and leave him hanging. It was his body language, the way he leaned closer to me, the way he squinted just a little, trying to figure out what I was going to say in response.

"Dave, no," I breathe, but he cuts me off before I can finish whatever thought I had.

"It's perfect. You know as well as I do that they're not going to stop." With his free hand, the one not squeezing the life out of mine, he stabs his finger on the blackmail letter. "They got your earrings, and now they want this money. It's escalating. What could they possibly want next?"

I shake my head, wanting to ignore his words, wanting him to stop talking, but at the same time I know he's right.

On some twisted level, somehow, he's right.

"Stop denying it, Mom." There's the sharp edge to his words again. "You've seen movies. Read books. What's the only way to stop a blackmailer?"

"Blackmail them," I offer, hopeful. "We know they're not scrupulous, not if they're willing to hide the truth about a murder so they can get what they want. I'm sure they'd have some skeleton hidden in their closet, and all we have to do is find out what it is. That won't be hard."

I'm warming to the idea now. It sounded a little silly at first, even I'm willing to admit that, but it's a good idea. There's no reason why it can't work.

"What are you talking about?" Dave's face twists in disgust, like he can't believe I'd be so stupid. "No, that's not what we do at all. They're not going to stop, and, what, we want this to turn into a game of who can blackmail the other worst? No, Mom, that's stupid."

I didn't think it was stupid, but I fall silent anyway.

"We *take care of them*. Kill them."

"Don't say that." I look around the yard, suddenly terrified someone might be out there. Watching. Listening. "Dave, that's not an okay thing to joke about."

"Who's joking? We kill them, and there's no problem. No blackmail. No worry about someone crawling out of the woodwork five, ten, fifteen years from now and holding it over our heads. You said it yourself, Mom. I'm not the only one who would get in trouble now. You're in it with me."

I can't breathe. Slowly I lift my eyes to look at my son. He's not the baby I cried over when I was seventeen when having a child. He's a man now and determined to make his own decisions, no matter how terrible I think they might be, no matter how much danger they put him, and me, in.

If I squint, though, I still see him, still see my little boy. He's in there, in Dave. And he's scared.

"Dave, there's got to be another way," I say, but he's standing, shaking his head. My son towers over me on a good day, when he's just standing next to me, but now? With him standing and me sitting on the porch? I feel like the roles are reversed, like I'm a little kid being scolded for doing something I did wrong.

"You know as well as I do that there isn't any other way, Mom. If there were, you would have already come up with it, am I right?"

I don't respond.

"We'll gather up our money," he says, and now he's gaining momentum. He looks excited, like this is the best thing that could have happened to him, like he's honestly looking forward to what's about to happen. "We'll pool it, what you and I each have, and that will give us enough. And then we'll make the drop."

"Dave, you can't just kill someone in the park," I argue, but he's no longer here with me. His body is here on the porch, but his mind is elsewhere. He's at the park already, hunting the person who would dare do this to us, fully prepared to do whatever needs to be done.

"Not at the park," he tells me with a scoff. *How can you be so stupid, Mother?* "That would be insane. Elsewhere, though. We'll follow them. I'll end this."

25

THURSDAY

I ended up calling in sick yesterday, although I was loathe to lie and say it was the flu. The last thing I wanted was for Richard to penalize me and keep me out of work longer than I needed. So I told him it was a migraine. I had them when I was younger, and I remember the splitting pain, the way sound and light work together to turn every breath into the most painful experience. It was easy for me to lie, to tell him I had to be in bed. Richard didn't like it, but he didn't have to like it.

He believed me, or said he did, and that was the only thing that mattered. It meant I could take care of Dave's school issue and still keep my job. Rather than calling Principal Byler and falling on my sword for her forgiveness, though, I sucked it up and simply filled out the required paperwork, then took Dave to the remedial school for his first day.

He can still ride the bus, thank goodness. Otherwise, I don't know what I'd do. Getting him to school and then getting myself to work has been hard enough, but now that he's going to go to school on the other side of the county?

There's only so much I can do.

But that was yesterday. Now I stumble onto my front porch, exhausted from work. It's silly to think Richard punished me for taking yesterday off, but I swear, the diners I had today were some of the pickiest, meanest, and lowest-tipping people I've ever waited on. Even Carla noticed and felt bad for me. She offered to split her tips with me, but I refused.

I'm not a charity case, no matter how much Dave and I could use that extra money. It's easy to accept help from people, but then you always have to pay them back.

I'm not getting sucked into that spiral.

My key slips into the lock, and I take a deep breath before pushing the door open. My nerves are frayed, and I strain my ears, listening for any sign of my son. He should have been dropped off by the bus hours ago. He should be here. If he's not...

"Hi, Mom." Dave sounds happy. His voice comes from the kitchen, and I drop my purse, lock the door behind me, then head there. I don't know what I'm expecting, but it's not what I see.

"You made dinner?" Somehow I keep the surprise out of my voice. "Thank you."

"It's not much," he says, raising his shoulder in a shrug. "We really need to go to the store, but I found some Spam and made fried Spamwiches. There was a can of fruit cocktail, so I opened that, and then I found some cookies you had stashed way back in the freezer."

"This is perfect," I tell him, and I mean it, but I'm not just talking about the food. I'm talking about all of it, his attitude, the fact that he so willingly went to school, how kind he's being. It's terrible that the blackmail letter has changed his behavior so much, but it's even worse that I enjoy it.

"Well, you do so much. And I thought it would be nice." He sits, gesturing for me to join him. "We don't want the sandwiches to get cold. The only cheese I could find was some old American slices, but there's ketchup if you want that. And hot sauce." He sounds nervous.

I sit across from him and take a sip of water. "How was school?"

"Actually pretty good. Can you believe I'm not the bad kid there?" I raise an eyebrow, and he continues, "I'm serious. Some of the kids there are really bad."

Are they also murderers?

"Well, just keep your head down and do your work," I say, like that's going to be enough to keep him out of trouble. "This isn't just a fresh start, Dave, it's your last chance."

"I know."

We fall to eating, both of us obviously hungry after the long days we had. I'm really enjoying dinner, even though Spam is my least favorite food. Partly because I'm just hungry after a long day on my feet, partly because food always tastes better when someone else makes it. It's science.

"I've been thinking about Saturday," he says casually, like he's talking about a movie he wants to go see.

My stomach drops. Flips. The Spam in it sits like lead. "Saturday?"

"The drop. That's when the note said to bring the money to the park. It's the same place I took your earrings."

I stare at him, looking for something. Remorse, maybe? But there's nothing there but focus. "Okay. What are you thinking?"

"That you make the drop. As soon as you do, you call me and let me know it's done. Describe the person to me. The park shouldn't be really busy that time of night. I'll have the car in the parking lot, and I'll follow them when they leave with the money. Then I'll end it."

My stomach curdles, and I push the rest of my food away. One more bite and I might throw up. "I don't think we have to kill them."

He leans forward, planting his hands on the table. "Mom, listen to yourself. Think about it."

"I am thinking about it. I'll pick up extra shifts at the diner. I'll get a second job elsewhere if I need to. There's no reason to rock the boat, no reason for you to..." My voice drops without me meaning for it to. "Kill someone." I pause. "Else."

You'd think I'd told him I was going to the police with information about George. Dave stiffens, his face drawing into a hard plane. "You can't be serious."

"It's better than killing someone. You have to see that." The more we discuss this, the more he continues down this path, the more I feel like I don't know him.

"This person owns us, Mom. Do you realize that? We belong to them. As long as they're walking around free, as long as they know the truth about what happened, we can't ever be free."

"No." I stand, slamming my hand on the table. The sound is loud, and it surprises both of us.

There's a flash of defiance on Dave's face—there and gone—and now he just looks impressed. Surprised, but impressed.

"We're not killing this person, Dave. I'm going to help

you make the drop, but you're not killing them on Saturday. We have to talk to them. Figure out what they want."

"Money. Earrings. More money." He's ticking items off on his fingers. "Money, money, money." Both hands are up now, and he stands. His face is turning red, his eyes dark. "You'd rather let this person walk all over us, let them take and take and take than let me handle it for you?"

"Dave, we can talk about this," I say.

But he shakes his head. "There's nothing to talk about. I'm willing to do whatever it takes to protect us. You aren't."

"That's not true," I say.

He's shaking his head harder now. He's acting like he knows what I'm going to say and has no interest in hearing it.

"Let me try to fix this first," I say, desperate for him to listen to me. "If I can't fix it, then we'll think about your way."

He pauses. It's like a balloon has popped, and he's slowly deflating, his shoulder curling in, his hands releasing some of the anger they held just a minute ago. "You promise you'll let me take care of it if you can't think of another way?"

"I promise."

He nods. Leaves the kitchen. Walks so quietly up the stairs that it would almost be possible for me to pretend this conversation didn't just happen, that he didn't seem excited about the prospect of ending this on his terms.

Now I just have to figure out what to do. Dave has a plan.

But I don't.

26

SATURDAY

Light from my bedroom window hits me in the face, and I roll over, groaning as I stretch my arms above my head. Man, it feels good to just exist in bed. My sheets are dirty, and I need to wash them today, but my bedroom is cool. Dave must have cranked up the AC before going to bed last night. While I'd normally be upset with him for doing that without talking to me about it, I can't deny the fact that it feels really, really good.

I always sleep better when it's cooler, and I can burrow under a thick layer of blankets like I'm a bear going into hibernation. The only problem with sleeping like this, though, is that I don't want to get up. I could stay like this forever, tucked under my blankets, the sound of birds chirping outside my window.

It's Saturday.

The thought hits me like a ton of bricks, and I sit up, a gasp ripping from my throat. All the enjoyment I felt over staying in bed and lounging a little is gone. Terror and angst battle for control as I throw my covers back and get out of bed. Before I can even pull on a bathrobe to go downstairs, however, there's a knock on my door.

"You decent?" Dave sounds hopeful. Excited. The exact opposite of how I feel right now.

"I am," I manage, tying the robe around me. I cinch it extra tight, like I'm putting on armor that will protect me from what's going to happen today.

"Great. I'm coming in." The door swings open, and Dave walks through carrying a tray loaded with food. There's toast and orange juice, sliced apple and scrambled eggs. My stomach rumbles, and he grins. "Coffee's perking. I can bring you up a cup when it's ready if you'd like."

"I'll come down for it," I say, taking the tray from him and putting it on the foot of my bed. "Thank you for this, but what's the special occasion?"

"I washed all the laundry and thought you'd like something to eat. I'm going to mow before it gets too hot. Is there anything else you need done around the house?"

I swallow hard. "No, that sounds great," I say. "Thank you."

"Okay, then I'm off. Remember, coffee is ready downstairs. I'll be back in later." He waves and leaves, closing my bedroom door behind him.

I slowly lower myself to my bed, careful not to knock over the orange juice. The fact that Dave made me breakfast and then took care of so many things around the house sits heavy on me. I'm in shock, I know I am.

"What do I do now?" I ask my empty room, knowing I won't get a response. It's hard for me to think when my brain is running a million miles a minute like this.

Dave's being blackmailed. Both of us could be in a lot of trouble if we're not careful, if we don't take care of this the right way. There might be a way to stop it, to end the blackmail, either through talking to the person or...or letting Dave take care of it.

But what if I like this Dave?

What if—and I know this is terrible to even think, let alone dwell on—I like Dave being so good? I like him helping out around the house, being willing to do things without being asked. I like him making me food and being quieter. I don't like that he's so fixated on killing the person blackmailing him, but I can handle that. I'm sure I can.

I don't know the last time my son made me this happy.

There he is, a little boy, running at me with a fistful of flowers. He's just picked them and seen a frog, and this is the best day of his life. I can see the green stems hanging down from his hand, his fist clenched tight around them so he doesn't drop them.

No. I shake my head, and that little boy is gone. He's been gone for years, but I still keep trying to get him back, to protect him, to make sure nothing bad happens to him. I'm sure a psychologist would have a field day talking to me about Dave. Even I know that I need to let him grow up, let him be the adult he is now, but I can't.

I still want to protect him. I want him to look at me with that same loving expression, like he can't believe how lucky he is that we have each other, like he's in awe of the world around him. But he's not in awe, he's hard and jaded, and right now the only thing keeping him good is the threat of going to jail.

Blackmail. That's the only thing making sure my son is a good person.

The smell of breakfast turns my stomach. I should eat something so I have the energy to get through whatever this day brings, but the thought of food right now is enough to make me feel sick. Ignoring the tray, I hurry to the bathroom to get ready.

Half an hour later I'm dressed and as ready for what the day will bring as I can be. Carefully, so I don't spill, I carry the breakfast tray back downstairs and dump everything in the trash. The last thing I want is for Dave to realize I didn't eat any of it and get angry with me. Not that I've seen that anger in a while, but it's there. Simmering.

The lawnmower eats through the grass. Dave walks behind it with a Zen expression on his face. He looks... happy, and I pause at the living room window, pressing my hand against it as I watch him. I can't remember the last time he mowed without me practically begging him to. He's never been one to take initiative around here, to just step up when I need him to, and I have to admit—I like it.

"I could get used to this," I say, then walk back into the kitchen to pour myself a cup of the coffee he made. This will give me the boost of energy I need to make it through my late morning shift at the diner and then whatever else this day brings. Carla's opening, so I can come in later today. Dave will wear himself out working in the yard, he'll feel accomplished and helpful, and then the two of us can talk about what we're going to do once I get back home.

We have to give the blackmailer the money. That's what we agree on, but after that, we can't come to an agreement. Dave is so dead set on killing the blackmailer that it terrifies me. A month ago I never would have thought Dave could kill a person.

Threaten them? Sure. Beat them up if they upset him? Definitely. He's gotten into more fights than I can count but never pulled a weapon, never even put the other person in hospital. He's always showed restraint, always kept his temper in check so nobody got seriously injured.

And then it all changed with George.

A chill races up my spine, and I turn on the hot water to wash the dishes. Keeping busy is key right now; it will ensure I don't go crazy while I try to figure out what to do.

Soap bubbles fill the sink, and I plunge my hands in, grateful for the heat.

I really think I can talk to the blackmailer and convince them to leave us alone. I know Dave wants to end them, wants to make sure they can't come back and hurt us in the future, but that's being rash. He has to trust me. Has to believe that I can take care of this.

"And if that doesn't work, Anne Marie? What then? How far are you willing to go to protect your son?"

I don't have to answer that question.

I already know what I'd do for Dave.

27

In the end, no matter how much I would have liked to stay, I have to go to work, have to leave Dave at home. It makes me antsy, thinking about him in the house by himself, but I stop my thoughts from getting away from me. *What's the worst he could do?* It's laughable, isn't it, that I would be worried about him alone in the house when I know what he's planning?

Still, once I park my car in the back parking lot of the Early Bird, I take a minute to pull up his location on my phone. Dave doesn't know he's sharing his location with me and would probably—*definitely*—be angry with me if he knew, but it's just better this way.

Not that I check it very often, but it's a nice safety blanket to have. If I'm honest with myself, I don't check it regularly because I don't want to know where he is. It almost seems better to not know, to imagine him behaving, not getting in trouble, than to know the truth.

But now I want to know—*I need to know*—and my muscles all tense as I tap his little icon and wait for the screen to reload. It does after a minute, the spinning wheel of death finally disappearing, and I exhale hard in relief.

He's at home, right where he's supposed to be. He promised me he'd stay home all day long, and so far he is. Relief makes my shoulders sag forward, and I watch the screen for a minute, half expecting it to refresh and him to be at Jeremy's house or in some other unapproved location.

It doesn't, and I turn off my phone, gratitude flowing through me as I get out of my car and walk to the staff door in the back of the building. Richard likes us to come in through the back so none of the diners see us before we're all ready to start working unless we're the opening shift. He says there's nothing worse than getting people's hopes up about getting their food and then not deliver because we're not yet on the clock.

Hate to argue with him, but there are a few things I can think of that are way, way worse.

"There she is!" Carla's in the middle of restocking her apron pocket with a new notepad but stops long enough to throw me a grin. "How are you doing, Anne Marie?"

"Just fine, Carla." I manage to smile at her even though all I want to do is go home. Go back to bed. Rewind a few weeks so none of this happened. "You?"

"Great." She adjusts her name tag even though it looks perfect to me. "Tell me, what are you and Dave up to this evening? Any good plans?"

I freeze. "Nothing planned, I don't think," I say. If she were to look at my calendar, she'd think that was true. There's nothing written down for Saturday, because what am I supposed to write? *Pay off blackmailer, 8 pm*?

Yeah, I think not.

"Well, I don't have anything going on, and I'd love to

hang out if you're free. I think we both get off at four, so we can totally get together if you want."

"Thanks," I tell her, my brain racing as I try to come up with an excuse that will keep her as far away from our house as possible.

Oh, hi, Carla, come on in. What's this? Drug money? Oh, no, we're just counting out two thousand dollars so the blackmailer who knows my son killed someone will leave us alone for just a bit longer. Next they might want my car. Or the house, who knows?

"Hey, are you okay?" Carla puts her hand on my shoulder. "You look pale. Like you don't feel so good."

"Oh, I'm fine," I tell her, trying to laugh. "Dave made breakfast this morning, and I think maybe the eggs aren't sitting the way they should."

"He made breakfast?" She mock gasps, covering her mouth with her hand. "I never thought I'd live to see the day."

"He's a good kid, Carla." I pull my apron on over my head and tie it behind my back as quickly as possible. "I don't think people give him enough credit. There's nothing wrong with Dave."

"Surely not," she agrees. "You're his mom, so you know best. I bet, in that teeny little house of yours, it must be about impossible to keep any secrets from each other. Am I right?"

"Pretty much." Does my voice sound light? Unaffected? I need to make sure she doesn't suspect anything. Carla's incredibly nosy, and if she gets even the littlest sniff that something is going on with Dave, I'm sure she'll hound me until she finds out the entire truth.

And that's not something I can have happen.

"Well, you're so lucky. Actually, now that I think about it, I know so many women...single moms who have problems with their kids. Sons, in particular. It's like they just really need a father figure, you know? Or who knows how they'll turn out? But I'm so glad Dave isn't an issue. You got lucky, Anne Marie."

I hate her. I have to force myself to smile and not scream right in her face. "So lucky," I parrot, then grab my notebook. "Have a good shift, Carla. I'll talk to you later."

And with that, I put her behind me.

I have so many other things to worry about, and I refuse to let Carla be one of them.

28

"This is what's going to happen. You're going to stay in the car, out of sight, completely hidden. I'll make the drop and try to see who comes to get it."

Dave shifts position next to me in the passenger seat but doesn't say anything.

We've argued about this to the point where I'm blue in the face, but I still feel like we need to hash it out. I need to make sure he's on the same page. This really isn't something we can half-ass.

"I'll call you after they pick up the drop, but chances are really good they'll be dressed all in black, or with a skullcap on, or something. We have to assume they'll have a gun, so you can't approach them. Do you understand?"

He nods, but his jaw is so tight, the muscles popping out, that I know he's not happy with me.

"I need to hear you say it, Dave. I need you to promise that you won't try to approach this person. We let them go tonight."

"And then what? They'll just come at us again. You know that, right?" Each word is hard, clipped, the edges of them painful to my ears.

"Promise me, Dave."

He heaves a sigh. Works his jaw.

I'm sitting patiently, the car keys still in my hand, unwilling to even start the vehicle before I know that we're on the same page.

"Fine. I promise. We'll let this person rob us blind and—"

"And we'll figure out our plan of action after we know who they are," I finish for him. "There's no other good way to do this. If we act on emotion, on impulse, then it's entirely possible one or both of us will get hurt. We have to assume they're armed, or that someone knows what they're doing. There might be more than one of them."

I'm squeezing the keys so hard they dig into my skin, but I don't look away from Dave, don't loosen my grip. He has to see how important this is, and I don't think he gets it yet.

"If you let me call someone, I could get us a gun."

I bark out a laugh. "Absolutely not. Now, I need you to agree, or we're going to miss the drop altogether. That's the last thing either of us want."

"Fine. I agree. I'll sit in the car like a neutered lapdog, doing whatever you think is best, *Mother.*"

I ignore his barbs and start the car, taking my time as I turn around and drive out to the main road. How terrible would it be if we were to get in an accident on the way there? We'd be late, and without a way to contact the blackmailer, they might think we hadn't done as asked.

And they'd take Dave from me.

A lump forms in my throat, and I swallow it. "You have the money?"

"Right here." He pats a bag at his feet. "Are you sure I can't make the drop? I—"

His words are cut off as I slam on the brakes, bringing us to a dead stop in the middle of the road. "Don't try to change the plan, Dave."

"Right. Sorry." He glares at me as he massages his chest where the seatbelt caught him. "You don't have to be involved if you don't want, Mom. That's all."

"You involved me the day you hit our neighbor." I start driving again, keeping my eyes on the road. I'd love to look at his face and work out what he's thinking, but the most important thing is for me to avoid an accident. Avoid a cop. Go the speed limit and hope nothing bad happens between here and the park.

And it doesn't. It takes us fifteen minutes to get there, which means I don't have a lot of time to make the drop. "Stay here," I tell Dave, then force myself to hand him the keys. I'd take them with me, but if this goes south and he needs to leave, I want him to be able to escape. "Wait for me. In the car, okay? I'll call you when the drop gets picked up, but I don't want you doing anything stupid." I pause, thinking. "I trust you, Dave."

"Got it. You trust me." He takes the keys and hands me the bag of money.

It's slimmer than I would have thought, considering it has all of our combined savings in it. After getting out and closing the door, I flip my hood up over my head, yanking tight on the cords to cinch it around my face. The last thing I want is for anyone to recognize me. A black hoodie and blue jeans shouldn't look too suspicious, right?

Taking a deep breath, I hurry into the park. We're the only car here, but I know there's another lot on the other side. This one is closest to our house, and I have to hope the park is empty, that people are home getting ready for bed.

Crickets chirp from the grass. I pass an abandoned kickball, left in the middle of the path, and I sidestep it, focused on my end goal. I'm supposed to leave the money by the covered bench at the lake. Wisteria drips from the pergola over the bench, creating a curtain around anyone sitting there. I'll drop the money and hurry back out, doing my best to make sure I look like I'm really leaving.

Only I'm not, am I? Instead of making my way back to the car, which is what I really want to do, I'm going to jump off the trail and tuck myself behind a tree. Dusk is falling faster and faster, and I have to hope that whoever our blackmailer is, they won't see me there.

But I'll see them.

I reach the bench and put the money down, taking time to look all around me. It's an exaggerated motion, one I hope the blackmailer sees. Goosebumps break out down my arms as I think about them watching me, but I can't do anything about that right now.

They have the upper hand for now, but I'll have it soon enough.

It's a gut-wrenching feeling, walking away from so much money, but I do it, hurrying down the path. Once I've turned a bend and am far enough away from the bench to feel comfortable, I leave the trail. Get into the trees.

Slowly work my way back.

Each twig underfoot makes me jump. I slow when I trip on an exposed root, then go faster when I check the time.

Any minute now.

Finally, I'm close enough to see what's going on, and I kneel, my eyes straining against the dying light. When I came up with this plan, I hadn't really taken into consideration how terrible the light would be, but I'm not backing out now.

And then I see them. The blackmailer hurries to the bench. There they stop and look around in a parody of what I did when I left the money. I watch as they pick up the bag. Heft it.

They stop, kneeling on the ground with the bag, and unzip it. A moment later a flashlight clicks on so they can see inside, make sure there really is money there. The flashlight jerks up and hits them in the face. It's just a second, just a moment of illumination before they angle the light away. But it's long enough.

I know who it is.

29

My hands are shaking so bad that my fingers slip from the door handle once, twice, three times before Dave leans over and opens the door for me. I throw myself into the driver's seat and fumble the key into the ignition.

"You didn't call me," he accuses, holding his phone up in my face like he needs to prove that it never rang. "I sat here and waited and waited, and you never called! I almost came to get you! I thought something happened to you!"

His words are so loud in the small of the car that I put my hands over my ears and press down, closing my eyes and biting down on my tongue. Pain shoots through my body, but I don't let up, not until the throbbing in my tongue is so severe I'm worried I might bite it off.

"What's wrong with you?" He grabs my shoulder and gives me a shake.

I finally turn to look at him, dropping my hands from my ears as I do.

"What happened out there? I knew your plan was crap. I should have gone. You ruined it."

"I didn't ruin anything," I say, finally finding my voice. "You have no idea what happened out there, but it wasn't my fault. I didn't do anything wrong."

"What was it?"

I ignore him and crank the car, saying a little prayer when the engine finally catches. Throwing my arm over the back of his seat, I reverse out of the parking space, then tear out of the parking lot. A speed-limit sign flashes in the corner of my vision, but I can't seem to slow down.

I need to get away from there. Away from the park, away from what I just saw. It's silly to think that pressing my foot down harder, as hard as I can, on the gas will erase what I just saw, but I do just that, taking turns at insane speeds.

"You need to slow down, Mom." Dave grabs my arm. Squeezes.

When I turn to look at him, I'm shocked at the fear on his face, and I let up on the gas. "Sorry," I mumble.

"What happened back there? Did they see you? Did you talk to them?"

He's desperate for information, and it's not fair that I'm not giving it to him, but I still need time to work through what I just saw. It doesn't make any sense. It completely upends everything we were planning.

"I didn't talk to them," I say finally, knowing I need to give Dave some information or he's only going to grow more and more agitated. He's like a little kid, where you need to feed them tidbits or they'll only keep picking at you, only keep digging until they get what they want.

"Okay. That's good." He exhales, sits back in his seat. "Did they see you?"

I shrug. That I honestly don't know.

"But you saw them?"

I nod.

"And you didn't call me?"

"No. I was afraid they would hear me. It was so quiet in the park, and nobody was there. The last thing I wanted was for them to hear me talking to you and look over and see me. If they knew I was on the phone, then who knows how they might have reacted."

"That makes sense." He nods, then leans his head back against the headrest. "You're right, that could have been bad."

"So bad." We drive under a streetlamp, and bright light illuminates the car for a moment. I risk a glance at my son. It's a snapshot, barely enough time to soak in any details about him, but I do my best. I manage.

I see the way his lashes rest against his cheeks. How he chews on his lower lip, something he's always done when really upset about something. I see how he tightens his fingers against his thigh.

And then the light is gone. I can still see him move, see him nod or shake his head, but those little details of my son, the ones I cling to like they're going to be enough to bring him back to me, are gone. Lost in the dark.

"You're upset." His voice breaks the silence in the car.

It's an observation, not a question, but I still feel like I need to respond to him, like he's looking for some information from me, and I need to give it to him.

I clear my throat. "You're being blackmailed. Of course I'm upset."

"No, it's something more."

Silence, now, while I turn off the main road that will take

us out of town. One thing I hadn't considered was how long this drive with Dave would feel as we worked our way back home. I hadn't thought about the thick silence that would fill the car, pregnant with expectation and fear. I never once imagined that sitting this close to Dave for so long would fill me with worry.

Because I could tell him who I saw, couldn't I? It would be easy, and I know my son. He'd take care of it, faster than I'm ready for him to do. He'd demand I drop him off where he could handle it right now, before it goes any further.

He'd bring back my money. And my earrings, if they hadn't been sold.

That almost makes it sound tempting, doesn't it?

But he'd be so filled with rage that he'd act out. Be stupid. Do something irreversible, and maybe leave his DNA behind while doing it.

No, as much as I want this to be over, I can't allow Dave to take the wheel on this one. He's too reactive, and it would be bloody, messy.

Knowing who the blackmailer is, I really think I can fix this. I just need a chance to do that. I need the opportunity to sit down with them, tell them how they're hurting not just my son, but me. Tell them that Dave is sorry, that he never meant to hurt the neighbor, that it was all a mistake.

Maybe, if I do that, I can fix this.

Without getting Dave involved.

"I was scared," I finally say, slowing down for a stop sign and turning to look at Dave. "I was really, really scared, Dave. I didn't know if they'd find me, didn't know if there would be more than one person there, didn't know if they would beat the bushes looking for me hiding." I take a deep breath. My voice shakes. "I'm sorry I didn't call you, I knew I needed to, but I was so scared."

Press the gas. Turn my head away from my son so he can't read every emotion on my face.

"I never should have let you do that," he says, his voice quiet. "I know you had to be so scared, Mom. I'm sorry."

I nod, not trusting myself to say anything.

Did it work?

Can I have my sweet Dave back for longer this time? Will the threat of more blackmail to come hanging over his head keep him quiet and kind, willing to follow directions?

Yes. It has to. This is who Dave is. I know it. I don't care that he's been acting out. Now that he sees how good he can be, and I see how good he can be, I'm sure we can stick it out together.

"It's okay. I just want us to be happy. To be good. I like you going to school and helping out around the house, Dave. I like not getting in trouble at work. Can you just be good?"

"I can." He takes my hand. Squeezes it.

I like driving with two hands on the wheel, but I don't pull away from him as I turn onto our road. It's pitch black here, and I go slowly, my headlights slicing through the dark. A few times I see the illumination of eyes looking back at us from the woods, and I shiver, wondering what's out there.

We pass George's old house. Then Carla's.

I don't let myself look at hers.

I can't give Dave any opportunity to realize she's who I saw in the park.

30

SUNDAY

Sunday morning and I'm off. Dave's outside reading, which is something I don't think I've seen him willingly do in years. It's strange to watch him out there, barely moving except to turn a page or lift his coffee to his lips. I stand still in the window for a while, just watching, unable to look away from my son.

I blink, and there he is, a little boy, flipping through a picture book. I can see the way the sun shines on his head, how he swings his feet, unable to touch the ground. He loves that chair out there, loves the bright blue pillow I bought on sale at Walmart, and has told me over and over again that he could live out there with the frogs and the worms.

A smile plays on my lips, and I touch the window, considering for a moment if I should go out there and talk to him.

Another blink and the little boy is gone. Dave's feet rest firmly on the ground. The blue pillow is still there, right behind his back for lumbar support, but it's faded. I should probably throw it away, get a new one when the summer sale starts in a few months, but it's insane to even think about spending money on something like a pillow when we just paid two thousand dollars to keep a blackmailer off our backs.

No, not a blackmailer. *Carla.* I don't have to dig deep to remember the fear and anger that ripped through me when I recognized her. She was the one who'd seen Dave. She'd been the one to come to work with me and pretend nothing had happened.

I grit my teeth, pain shooting up into my jaw.

How could she?

Sure, she drives me nuts from time to time, and we can step on each other's toes at work, but I trust her. *I thought I trusted her.*

Until she started looking out solely for herself.

The thought hits me like a ton of bricks. How could Carla, the woman I consider...well, not a *friend*, exactly, maybe I'm lying to myself when I say that we're that close, but someone I trust well enough to cover my back at work, turn on me like this? How could she look me in the eyes and pretend everything was fine, like she's got my back, like she would never do anything to hurt me, then blackmail my son?

I think of all the times she's stood up to Richard for me, all the times she's helped me out at work by covering a table when I was busy or switching shifts with me if I needed to.

I honestly thought I could trust her. And now she does this to me?

The betrayal, on top of what Dave did, makes me feel sick. I spin away from the window, unable to look at my teenage son any longer. I want him to be little again so I can protect him from all the evils of the world. That's been my one goal as his mother, to keep him safe, and I'm failing at that.

The thought crosses my mind that I shouldn't have to protect him from what he did, that him killing another person is the worst thing he could have done, but I push it away. Dave made a mistake, that much is true. I'd never try to argue against that or deny that he shouldn't have done what he did.

But he doesn't deserve to have it held over his head for the rest of his life. He doesn't deserve to be worried every second of the day that someone will be there, watching, taking note, doing whatever they can to hurt him. Nobody deserves that, especially not my son.

My heart slams in my chest. I'm going to have to come clean with Dave about who the blackmailer is, but maybe I can wait a little bit longer. I know I've failed my son in the past. I haven't been the best mother I could have been. I haven't made sure that he was always on the straight and narrow.

I know that.

And I know he doesn't deserve what's happening to him right now, but I can't help but appreciate how good he's been. How kind. Thoughtful. It's crazy to think that the blackmail might not all be bad, that I can look for some good in it.

But that's exactly what I'm doing right now.

How many times have I threatened him? Threatened to take away the car, to go to his teacher, to stop giving him money when he asks, and he's just laughed it all off. Like he knew I wouldn't actually do anything. Like he knew I was full of hot air and nothing bad would happen to him.

But now the threat against him is real. And he's being the

best he's ever been. I shouldn't rejoice in that, shouldn't be happy that there's finally enough fear in his life for him to pay attention, for him to change and be good.

But it's nice.

Pushing other thoughts about what will happen when the threat of the blackmail disappears, I walk outside to see Dave. He's my son. I love him. I want to spend as much time with him as possible, especially when he's in a good mood.

He looks up at me, his fingers working the edge of the page like he's antsy to turn it and find out what happens next in the story, and he smiles.

"Hi," I say, sitting next to him. "How's the book?"

"Good." He closes it but keeps his finger in the pages so he doesn't lose his spot. "What's going on?"

"I was going to run to the grocery store today, but our grocery budget took a bit of a hit." I smile to lessen the impact of the words. *It took a hit because you killed someone, Dave. Don't forget that.*

"There's tuna in the cupboard," he says, standing. "And I saw pasta. A bit of milk. I'll come up with something. You can spend some time doing whatever it is you want, okay? Let me take care of lunch."

"Thanks." I grab the blue pillow and put it behind my back for a little support before leaning back and closing my eyes. The sun feels good on my face. The day stretches out ahead of me, full of purpose and excitement, and I'm not going to look this gift horse in the mouth.

I know we need to deal with Carla. And I will, I promise. I won't let her take my son from me.

But right now I want to sit in the sun. I want to have time to think about what to do.

And I want to enjoy the new Dave. New and improved. *Dave 2.0.*

And all it took was someone dying.

31

MONDAY

Monday morning sees me back to work. For the first time in a while, I don't check my phone to make sure Dave headed in to school. I'm honestly not worried about him skipping or doing something stupid. He has his head on straight, just like he did after the first blackmail letter.

My only question is how long will it last?

I'm retying my sneakers to make sure I don't trip on the laces while carrying a tray full of food when the door to the back room opens and Carla slips inside. She throws me an easy grin and closes the door behind her before sagging against it.

"I just had the best weekend ever," she tells me.

I feel myself stiffen. I knew it would be difficult to come here and listen to her talk about what she did with my money, to think about her wearing my earrings, but it's harder now that she's here, her perfume burning my nose, her giggles making me want to clamp my hands down over my ears.

"What did you do?" I ask, because that's what any normal person in a normal situation would ask someone they work with. They wouldn't stare, or roll their eyes, or shove them out of the way to flee the room, which is what I really want to do.

"Took myself out for brunch on Saturday and Sunday," she says, grinning. "And then I went shopping at the new outlet malls Sunday afternoon. It was amazing to have a little extra spending money."

She's really rubbing it in, isn't she?

"Did you win the lottery or something?" I ask. It's difficult for me to keep a smile on my face, but I manage. "Sounds like your weekend was pretty pricy."

"It was, but it was worth it," she tells me, completely glossing over where she got the money. "Anyway, enough about me. What did you and Dave get into?"

"Mostly stayed home," I tell her, which is true because of the money she stole from us. "Worked in the yard. Read. Dave made lunch, and we spent a fair amount of time just quiet in the house." I'm desperate to make her see how good my son really is.

"They do say boys mature later than girls."

I shrug and stand, moving closer to her so she has to step away from the door and let me out. "I guess so. It was bound to happen sooner or later."

"So no big life event?" She's hot on my heels, practically panting down my neck.

I have a sudden and intense mental image of whipping around, grabbing her by the neck, pushing her into the wall. My fingers would sink right into her soft neck, and she'd mewl, grabbing at them to try to break my grip. God, it would feel good to just keep squeezing as her face slowly turned purple.

I've watched enough movies to know her eyes would bug out. Her lips would swell. Even if I couldn't see it, her tongue would thicken in her mouth until it was more like a gag than anything, stopping the pathetic little noises she was making. I can just see my hands gripped around her throat, the refusal to give up coursing through my veins.

I blink.

Carla is still behind me. In front of me, the wall, empty of any people being strangled. I feel the hair on the back of my neck stand up, and I turn around slowly, half expecting Carla to have bloodshot eyes, to be panting and gasping for air, for her hands to be reaching for my face so she can push me off her.

"No," I manage, shaking my head. "No big life event. You said it yourself, that boys mature slower than girls, you know."

"They also say that boys will be boys, but I believe boys will be held accountable for their actions."

Oh, it's like this, is it?

"By a judge and jury of their peers, sure." I tuck some rogue hair behind my ear. "Thank goodness we live in a country with such a great justice system."

"Great justice system." She scoffs. "My father was killed by a drunk driver when I was a little kid, have I ever told you that, Anne Marie? It was terrible. My mother started drinking immediately and drank herself to death. My little brother and I were left to fend for ourselves."

"That's terrible. I'm so sorry you went through that."

"Me too. And do you want to know what's worse?"

I don't. Partly because I have a feeling I know where this

is going, partly because I want this conversation to be over. I never should have let her bait me into it. She's smarter than me, I know she is.

"What's worse is what happened to the drunk driver." She rubs one eye like there's something in there. "Nothing. Nothing happened to him. He got some sleazebag lawyer, and the guy managed to get off. We'd see him at the store sometimes, you know. Shopping. For beer."

My mouth goes dry. There are so many conflicting messages in what she just said that I don't know what to do.

"The justice system failed your father," I tell her. "I'm sorry about that."

"Not as sorry as I am." She sniffs, wipes her hand on her apron. "Anyway, I just think we need to hold each other to higher standards, that's all. I'm glad Dave is finally figuring out how to be a productive member of society." She stares at me like she's considering what else she could—or should—say. Finally, "I like you, Anne Marie. You got dealt a crappy hand."

"It's looking up," I manage.

"Well, I'm glad." She puts her hand on my shoulder.

I have to fight the way my skin crawls. I want to step back from her so she can't touch me, but there's no way she wouldn't think that was weird. We're not super touchy-feely people, but she's touched me before and I haven't recoiled. I can't start now. "Thanks. You're a good friend."

Something flashes across her face, but the emotion is gone before I can put my finger on it. She grins at me, showing me more teeth than seems necessary. "You have no idea how good a friend I can be, Anne Marie."

32

FRIDAY

The week passes without incident. I have Friday afternoon off, and I take the leisurely way home from work, driving along the river instead of through town. It'll add twenty minutes to my drive time, but I don't really care. How long has it been since I've felt this relaxed or at ease?

Too long. From the moment I found out I was pregnant and knew I couldn't possibly raise my baby with Dave's dad, I've operated with a certain level of stress. Some people find stress to be revitalizing. They thrive under it, using stress to help them become the best they can be, but not me.

It eats at me. It wears away my sharp edges, making me feel dull and uninspired. It's crazy to think that stress can turn you into a shell of the person you were before, but I swear that's what's happening to me. Now, though, with everything working out with Dave, with my job finally under control, I feel like I'm turning back into myself.

My bright colors aren't back yet. I still feel a bit hollow and tired. But I'm turning more and more into Anne Marie every single day, and I like that. I like knowing that I'm finding myself again.

The plastic I taped over the broken window that Dave knocked out flaps as a breeze buffets the car, but I don't slow down. I've always judged people who drove around with broken windows, who hadn't got them fixed, but now that I'm that person, I can see how easy it is to ignore the problem.

And, besides, it's not like I have the money to fix it. If I'd known Dave was selling drugs, I might have turned to him before to get help. He might have given me the cash we need to fix some things around the house...but I won't think about that. Dave's made a lot of poor decisions in the past, but I'm sure that's all over now. He's turned over a new leaf, as they say, and I couldn't be happier that it's happened.

I can overlook everything he did in the past.

There's a spot by the river that's pretty popular in the summer, but with school still in session, I'm thinking I'll have some alone time there, and I pull up, parking under a spreading oak that offers tons of shade. It's hot out, but here, down by the river, it feels cooler. I appreciate the breeze on my bare arms as I get out of the car and carefully shut the door behind me.

It feels criminal to slam the door and disturb the quiet of this place. The river laughs and babbles over rocks and around bends. I throw a stick in, watching with interest as it gets swept away to land in a snag of branches and leaves. The path along the river is shaded, and I head in that direction, away from the car, pleased to have found something to do for myself.

Nobody's here to bother me. Hell, nobody even knows I'm here. On a whim, I pull my phone out of my pocket and press the button to power it down, but then I stop. *What if Dave needs me?*

I know he's almost a grown man, and that at some point I'm going to have to stop living my life worried about him, but now is not the time. Leaving my phone on, I tuck it back in my pocket and walk on, stopping to look at some of the wildflowers growing along the side of the path as I go.

It's when I'm bending down, sniffing a yellow trout lily, that I hear noises from up ahead. Voices. People are coming down the path towards me, and while I know there's nothing to be worried about, I stand back up, smooth down my shirt. As a woman, there's always some concern when out and about and faced with a man.

I like being in crowds when passing men. It makes me nervous to be out here on the trail by myself.

The voices grow louder, and I debate turning back and hurrying to my car. The thought of running along the path, spurred by fear, makes me angry. No. You know what? I'm done running.

Straightening up, I continue walking down the path. Whoever is coming towards me grows louder, almost to the point where I wonder if they're yelling. There's a man's voice...no, two.

Two men.

Again I stop, unsure of what to do. It's silly, isn't it? To have every movement I make ruled by fear, by concern for what a man might do if he found me here alone? I hate it, and that hatred is what spurs me to keep walking.

"I'm just saying, you could make more money if you sold downtown. Why you make people meet you here instead of going to where the demand is, I don't know."

I know that voice. I can't put my finger on who it is, or where I've heard it before, but I know it, I'm sure of it.

"I like coming here because nobody knows me." The second man speaks, and this time he's close enough for me to recognize his voice.

"Dave?" I whisper my son's name, heat flushing my cheeks when I think about how upset he'll be to come face-to-face with me on the trail.

"But the money!" The first voice again.

I swear I know it, I can't—

"Jeremy, cut me a break. You don't think I'm making enough here?"

Jeremy? I told him to leave my son alone.

"I think you could make more. And quit taking time off, man."

"I'm back now, aren't I?"

They're right around a bend in the trail. I catch a glimpse of red through the trees and recognize it as the shirt Dave had on this morning. As much as I want to convince myself that my son isn't here, I can't hide from the truth.

Now I wish I'd turned back to my car. Or never come here in the first place. I'd give anything to not have to face my son right now, but my feet are still moving, and the two of them are coming towards me. Suddenly, in place of trees, there they are, huge smiles on their faces, turning and looking at each other like they don't have a care in the world.

Like Dave isn't supposed to be at school.

Like he didn't promise me he'd come right home.

Like I don't suddenly want to kill Jeremy for leading my son astray.

"Dave?" I speak first, unwilling to give him the opportunity to slip right by me. "What are you doing here?"

"Mom." Dave stops short in the path, his eyes darting to me, then to Jeremy, then back to me. "What are *you* doing here?"

"I came for a walk after my shift." I wait, giving him ample time to come up with a reason why he and Jeremy are here. Never mind the fact that I told Jeremy to stay the hell away from Dave.

"I didn't think I'd see you here." Dave's guilt is evident. It's written all over his face. "I'll see you at home."

"Go to the car, Dave." Even I don't recognize my voice. I sound confident. In control.

"What?"

"The car. It's in the parking lot. Go there and wait for me. I'm taking you home."

Jeremy raises his eyebrows.

"You can't be serious. I'm not some little kid you can—"

"Go now!" I'm panting and stare at him, willing him, no, *daring* him, to argue with me. His jaw drops open, and he scoots past me on the trail, leaving me with Jeremy. I wait until my son is gone, until he has to be out of earshot. Then, "What the hell are you doing with Dave?"

"Hey, lady." He holds his hands up, much like he did when he thought I'd pulled a gun on him. "Your son is old enough to make his own decisions about who he wants to hang out with. We're friends. Don't fight it."

"Does he know you were robbing us?"

"Water under the bridge." A smile, like a ferret. My stomach turns. "Dave told me he needed more cash, and I'm happy to help him out."

"By making him sell drugs."

"Making? No, you listen here." His hands tighten into fists, but then he exhales hard and relaxes them. "I'm not making Dave do anything. In case you haven't noticed because you're too busy hovering, he's perfectly capable of handling things on his own. He's a big boy."

"You need to stay away from him."

He barks out a laugh. "Oh, yeah? Or what? You going to call the police and tell them I was in your house looking for money? I'm sure they'd love to come search your place and find all the drugs Dave hasn't sold yet. Back off. Dave can work with me, and you can turn your head the other way so you don't know what he's doing."

I don't know what to say. How did he know exactly what I was thinking about doing? Calling the police seemed like a good idea, like the best way to keep this guy away from me and my son. But he's right, if I call them and they come to the house, they'll find Dave's drugs, however many there are.

And then I'll lose my son.

I won't lose my son.

"Dave's better off without you," I snap, mostly feeling backed into a corner. I don't know what else to say to this guy, how to get him to back off. "He doesn't need you."

"I think if you were honest with yourself, you'd find that the truth is Dave doesn't need you." He passes me, knocking into my shoulder as he does.

I stumble and have to catch my balance before turning to watch him saunter down the path.

Dave doesn't need you.

But this guy is wrong. Dave needs me.

And I'm not going to back down now.

33

"I didn't know you were selling drugs." The words spill from my lips, surprising me, but especially surprising Dave. He's sitting across from me at the kitchen table and looks up sharply, his fork still suspended halfway to his mouth.

"We needed money," he says simply, like that's a good excuse for what he's been doing.

"I have a real job," I counter. "I don't want you hanging around with that guy, and I really don't want you selling drugs."

Dave frowns, puts his fork down. When he thinks hard like this, I swear I can see his brain working overtime. He's trying to see this argument from every angle before it really kicks into high gear, but I've got it under control. I'm not letting him come out on top of this one.

"What's your plan when the blackmailer calls and tells us that we need to give them more money?"

"I'm going to talk to them." My heart slams in my chest, desperately trying to escape, and I take a sip of water. It's cool and refreshing, and I hold it in my mouth for a moment before swallowing.

"*Talk* to them?" His eyebrows crash together, and he shakes his head. "Not a chance, Mom. Why would they be willing to talk to you? You think they're just going to agree to stop?"

I don't know, but I don't admit that to my son. The other thing I don't want to admit to him is that I like how good he is when living under the threat of blackmail. I like how helpful and thoughtful he is when he thinks someone is watching, thinks they might hurt our family. It's terrible to want him to be better and to rely on blackmail for him to be good, but that's what I'm doing.

Still, now I know he can be good. He's proven it twice now, once with each letter we've gotten. There's nothing to say he can't choose to be good permanently, that it can't just become who he is. If he can choose to be good when he's afraid of what a blackmailer might do to him, to us, why can't he be good all the time?

That's what I want. I want Carla to back off. To let me have my son. It's a strange feeling, to realize I'm not really even mad at her for what she is doing.

Yes, I'm angry about the money. And my earrings. But she showed me a different side to my son, one I haven't seen before. She showed me that he's not all rough around the edges. He's good and kind and true, and I know he can be like that all the time.

But not if she's still hanging over our heads. Not if her blackmail is going to keep coming, going to make him do stupid things like sell drugs for money.

"I think they will," I say, and I can see an argument coming, so I speak faster, wanting to head it off at the pass.

"Dave, listen to me. I don't know if you've noticed, but you're different with the blackmail. You're kinder. You help out around the house more. I don't want you to go back to selling drugs to pay off this person. I want the kind Dave you've been recently."

He frowns. "You like me when I'm running scared?"

"I like you when the real you comes out," I correct. "When you don't feel like you have to impress anyone by being tough or dangerous. When you get to just be my son. That's what I like."

"What if that's not the real me? The scared me?" He's challenging me, just like he used to when he was a little kid and wanted ice cream before dinner. I remember how those arguments would go, how I used to think he would grow up to be a lawyer, fighting for the underdog in court.

"It is the real you." I reach across the table and take his hand, terrified at first that he's going to pull away from me, but he doesn't. He doesn't return the squeeze I give him, but I don't care about that. I just care that I get to make contact without him trying to pull away.

Dave shakes his head, but the movement is slow, and I convince myself it's because he's not sure if he believes himself, not that he disagrees with me.

"I want you to stop selling drugs," I say, and his eyes snap to mine. There's fight in them, I can see it, but I ignore it. "You don't need to do that, Dave, not when I can get the blackmailer off our backs. And selling drugs will only put you at risk of running into the cops. It's an easy reach for them to find out about George once that happens."

"How would they make that leap?"

I think about all of the cop shows I've watched over the years and how convinced I was that they would never find the bad guy. It doesn't matter how careful the bad guy is, though, they always mess up somehow. There's always something they do, some little mistake, that leads to them being caught.

"Does it matter? It's not worth the risk."

"Jeremy wouldn't let me get caught." He pulls his hand away from me, and I'm acutely aware that I'm losing him. "He's my best friend. There's no way he'd let me go down for something."

"He tried to rob us." Anger flares in me, and I'm suddenly willing to burn everything down. "What do you think about your friend now, Dave? I came home, and he was here, digging around for money you owed him. Is that a friend?"

"What? No, he wasn't. You're just saying that so I'll cut ties with him. Really cute, Mom."

"He was right there!" I stand and point at the cupboards behind me where I caught him digging around. "Why would I lie to you about this? He was there, and I told him to get out. I told him I'd call the cops and that he needed to stay away from you."

A beat, then Dave shakes his head. I'm sure he's gearing up for another argument until he speaks.

"If that's true, Mom, and not some lie you're telling me, then we need to take care of things with him."

It takes a minute for his words to sink in.

"Wait, what do you mean?"

"Take care of him. Stop him from turning against us. What if you succeed in getting the blackmailer off our backs? What then? We have another one? Jeremy turns against me?" His eyes are bright. He plants his hands on the table, hard, making our glasses rattle.

"No, you can't do anything to him," I say. Panic rips at my

throat as I realize where Dave's train of thought is taking him. "Dave, I'm serious. You can't go off on your own on this one. Leave Jeremy out of it. Just leave him in the past so he can't hurt us anymore."

"And what if he doesn't go quietly? He knows what I've been doing, Mom."

I don't want to look at my son. The words he's saying are bad enough, but that's not what's the most upsetting. It's the expression on his face, the excitement etched there. He looks happy about what he's saying, about the thought of hurting his friend.

When did my son turn into a monster?

The thought hits me hard, and I recoil, turning away from the table, wanting to get away not only from Dave, but from those words. They're taking up residence in my brain, already settling down, like a stray cat under the porch. Something you know you shouldn't allow to stay, but something you're not sure how to get rid of.

He's not a monster. He's my little boy, and he needs my help.

"Let me take care of the blackmailer," I say, forcing myself to turn back to face Dave. "I didn't tell you at first, but I know who it is. I know they'll talk to me, okay? I'll stop this. You cut things off with Jeremy. But you can't hurt him, Dave. You can't do anything to him that will make people suspicious, do you understand?"

For a moment I think he's not going to answer. The thought terrifies me, and I dig my fingers into my thighs, keeping my eyes locked on my son.

"I could handle him."

"No. You're good, Dave, don't you see that? Just tell him you're getting a job, a real job. Tell him there's no hard feelings but that you don't want to continue selling for him, that you can make more money working in an office after school. Or scooping ice cream, or…I don't know, waiting tables. I don't care what you tell him, and you don't even have to get a job, okay? I'll take care of the money and give you what you need."

"But the blackmailer will want more."

"No, they won't. Because I'm going to talk to them, okay? I'll handle it with her."

"Her?" His eyebrows fly up. "Who is it, Mom?"

Crap.

I don't want to tell him. I just want to handle this on my own.

"Don't worry about it, okay? I just want you to trust me that I'm going to get her to back off."

"I think we should kill her." Dave leans forward. "Have a clean slate. Get rid of everyone who has the power to hurt us."

"No. Dave, no. I'll handle this. The discussion is over." I haven't finished my dinner, but there's no way I can eat anything else, not with my stomach in knots like it is right now. I stand and start clearing the table, but I can feel Dave's eyes on me the entire time.

That's not what has me so upset. What bothers me more than anything is that he might be right.

I'll talk to Carla, see if I can get her to stop. But what if she doesn't? I have to have a plan for what to do about her, but I can't tell Dave.

Not if I don't want him to try to take care of the situation first.

34

MONDAY

I'm nervous, and I wipe my hands on my apron to dry them off. It's gross, and if Richard were to see me doing that, I'm sure he'd have a fit, but he's not here, he's out haggling with a supplier to try to get a better deal on onions.

Carla should be here, but she's late, almost like she knew today would be the perfect storm of me wanting to talk to her and Richard not being around to see that she's clocking in after the start of her scheduled shift. I hurry to the back door and push it open, scan the parking lot for her car, then let the door slam shut again.

She's not here yet.

There's a worry I have that Dave might have figured out who she is and done something to her, but that's insane. It was only Friday night that he found out I knew the person, and as driven as my son is, I highly doubt he could possibly put all the pieces together in that short period of time.

Besides, the last time I checked my phone, he was at home.

It's compulsive, me pulling my phone from my pocket to check again, but seeing the little dot with his name above it at our house makes me relax. He was quiet last night after dinner and still didn't want to talk about our conversation, which is fair. I really didn't want to, either.

All I know is that I told him to end things with Jeremy. I told him to trust me to talk to the blackmailer. But now she's not here, and I can't help but worry.

"Order up!"

The cook's voice cuts through my thoughts, and I wipe my hands on my apron one more time before hurrying to take the food to my first table. It's a slow morning, probably because it's so overcast, and I only have two tables to wait on. Normally I'd be happy to have all of their tips to myself, but I want Carla here.

"Here's your French toast," I say, setting a plate in front of a little kid, "and a southwestern omelet with hash browns for you." It has to be his mom, the woman eating with him. They have the same turned-up nose and way of smiling. I should leave them alone, refill the coffee for my other table, and check for Carla.

But I can't seem to walk away.

"Mother-son morning out?" I ask.

She looks up at me. I notice how she has to drag her eyes away from her son. He's across the table from her and already sawing at his French toast. "Yep. Just me and my little man."

My heart squeezes. "I have a son," I offer, "but he's a bit older than yours. I can still remember just what he was like when he was so little. Time sure goes by fast."

She's not interested, but she is polite. "How old is he?"

I'm about to tell her that Dave is sixteen, but I realize

how silly it is for me to even have started this conversation. She'll think I'm crazy for comparing my teenager to her preschooler. "He's seven," I lie. Seven was a great age for Dave. He wasn't getting in trouble regularly yet, and he still loved to snuggle with me before bed. "Such a sweet boy, too. Always does what I ask."

She's still smiling, but it's looking strained, like she can't wait for me to leave the two of them alone.

"Anyway, I'll let you get to it." I back away from the table. "Enjoy your food and let me know if you need anything else."

"Thank you," she says, but she's already back to paying more attention to her son than to me. I'm not offended; that's how it's supposed to be. Mothers are always supposed to pay more attention to their children. They're supposed to be willing to sacrifice whatever they have to in order to protect their children.

Hurrying to the back, I peek out the door once more in search of Carla's car. It's there, having just pulled up, and I watch as the headlights turn off and she opens the driver's door. Just seeing her here and knowing the conversation I'm about to have with her makes my heart beat faster.

She hoists her purse higher on her shoulder, locks her car. Looks around like she's waiting for someone, but then finally turns and walks to the building. For a moment I consider closing the door and stepping away from it so she doesn't realize I'm so eager to talk to her, but it's too late.

Her eyes land on my face, and her mouth twists a little to the side, like she isn't sure of what she thinks seeing me standing there. I wave, lifting my hand just a little, and she returns it. Smiles.

Good. See? Nothing is wrong. She doesn't know that I

know the truth. There's no way she has any clue that I saw her at the park. Maybe, if this had been the first time we'd run into each other after the drop, I'd worry about the expression on her face, but it's not. She thinks I'm clueless.

But that's about to change.

"Good morning," I say, throwing the door wide for her and bracing it with my hand as she walks past me. "How are you doing?"

"Fine." She smiles. "What's going on? Why are you holding the door for me? Are we slammed or something? I didn't see many cars in the front parking lot."

"No, not slammed. Richard isn't here right now, and I thought it would be nice to catch up with you a little." There go my hands again, turning into sweat bombs, and I wipe them on my apron.

"Catch up?" She hangs her purse on a hook and slips her apron over her head. A moment later she has her name tag pinned to it, and she looks at me. "What do we need to catch up on?"

"Just...life." I flap my hand in the air. "I just don't get a lot of time to really talk to you, you know?"

She pauses. I can almost see the gears in her head working overtime as she tries to figure out what I'm really saying.

"Okay. I thought we talked, but I guess maybe not as much as you might like. It is our job to stay busy and not just chat, you know. I don't want to get caught standing around chatting and not doing what we're supposed to be doing."

"No worries. Like I said, Richard isn't here." I turn, following her as she grabs her notepad and heads to the door that leads out into the kitchen. "Hey, do you have a second?"

She's not slowing down. Why isn't she slowing down so we can talk? I'm frustrated, but I swallow it back and reach out, lightly touching her arm to get her attention.

Carla tries to jerk away from me, but I lightly hold her arm.

When she turns to look at me, her eyebrows are raised, her cheeks pink. "I really need to get out there, Anne Marie. You know as well as I do how important tips are. The last thing I want is to miss out on some of them because we were talking."

"I know, I know. There's just something big I want to discuss with you. It's about Dave."

She knows I know. I swear she does. I see something in her eyes, something like triumph, but it's quickly replaced with fear. Her mouth drops open a bit, and she shakes her head.

"I need to get to my tables," she tells me, but I grip her arm tighter, refusing to let her go. She can't just walk away from me now, not when she and I have so much to talk about. It isn't fair.

"Do you wear them?" I change tactics, desperate for something that will get her attention.

"Wear what?" Her question is breathless. She sounds like she's choking. I should feel bad for her, should pity her for how afraid she is, but I don't. I don't because of the position she put me in, because of what she's doing to my son.

"My earrings."

35

Carla's mouth drops open, but she snaps it back shut, giving her head a little shake like she's been swimming and has water in her ear.

"I don't know what you're talking about." Each word is stiff, stilted, held up by fear.

"I think you do." I take a step closer. She *smells* like fear, which isn't something I've ever experienced before. It's fascinating. I sniff her, and she recoils.

"Anne Marie, you're freaking me out. Let go of my arm." She pulls back, jerking her arm hard against my grip, but I don't loosen it. I don't want her to go. I told Dave I was going to take care of this on my own terms, and if she walks away from me now, then I have no idea how I'm going to do that.

I'm not going to fail my son.

"Carla," I say, her name a warning, but before I get any farther, the door behind her flies open. Richard blows through it, his chest puffed out, his cheeks red. Like I've been burned, I drop my hand and step back from her.

"What the hell is going on back here? You two lovers or

something?" He glares at Carla, then at me. We're both shaking our heads, but he continues, "I have tables out there waiting for food. What the hell am I supposed to tell them? That my incompetent waitresses are making eyes at each other in the back? What kind of place do you think this is?"

"Carla was feeling faint," I say, looking him dead in the eyes. "I thought she was going to pass out."

"But I'm fine." Carla stands up a little straighter. "Anne Marie was here for me, but I'm fine."

"Good." Richard somehow manages to growl the word, but his eyes are still dark. Distrustful. "Get out there. No more talking between the two of you today, do you understand? I'm fed up with you two." He shakes his head. "Women."

Carla nods, and the two of us spill out through the door into the kitchen. The cook turns and looks at us, raising his spatula in greeting, but nobody says anything.

"Carla, I have to talk to you," I say, desperate to end this. I didn't mean to let it all out right here at work. It just spilled out of me, and now that the cat's out of the bag, I have to finish this. What if Carla gets upset and turns Dave in now?

I turn, look at the cast-iron skillet on the stove. If she threatens to do that, I could stop her. Grab the skillet. Bring it up, over my head, then down on her. It would be hot and heavy, but I could stop her and make sure she doesn't hurt Dave.

"Leave me alone." She hisses the words at me, and I take a step towards the skillet. I don't even realize I've moved, but her eyes grow wide. "Anne Marie, let me work. I need the money. You need the money." She looks past me at the door to the small back room. "Don't ruin this."

"After our shift, then," I say, following her into the dining area. Richard was right, the tables are filling up, and diners turn to look at the two of us. Some look unhappy; some just look hungry. "Please, after our shift."

"I'm working a double and closing. Leave. Me. Alone." She spins off to the right side of the dining area where her tables are waiting for her.

I stand for longer than I mean to, just watching her, then turn to the left.

Tonight. I'll come back and talk to her. She won't be able to avoid me forever, I'm sure of it. Carla holds the key to what happens with the rest of my life, the rest of Dave's life.

She was willing to turn this into a game, but what she doesn't realize is that she's not the only one playing any longer. I'm onto her.

I turn, and our eyes meet across the room. For a moment, I'm sure she's going to break eye contact, going to look away, going to hide from me, but she doesn't.

She shakes her head. She frowns. Mouths something.

I'm not afraid of you.

Oh, but Carla, you should be.

36

I sit in my car, listening to the sound of the engine quietly ticking as it cools. Dave's home, I can see him walking back and forth in front of the kitchen windows, but he hasn't come out to check on me and see why I'm still sitting out here, and I appreciate it.

I don't want to tell him that, just for a moment, I considered killing Carla. I thought about bashing in her head, how her blood would pool on the floor, how I would happily do it all just to keep her from hurting my son. I don't want to tell him that because all it will do is encourage him to take matters into his own hands.

He already wants to end things with the blackmailer. And I don't even want to think about what he wants to do to Jeremy.

A shiver races up my spine, and I get out of the car, standing in the bright sun for a moment before forcing myself to walk into the house. Carla's working a double today and closing tonight. She slipped up when she told me that because now I know where to find her.

I just want to talk to her. I shouldn't have broached the topic at work, and I realize that now. It was stupid. It was sure to backfire in my face, and it did. Spectacularly. But at least I know where she'll be tonight. I know I can get her on her own.

"How was work?" Dave eyeballs me like he's afraid I'm going to blow up at him, but I force a smile to my lips instead.

"Work was work," I say. "How are things around here?"

There are so many unspoken questions hanging in the air between us, but I can't voice them. To voice them would be to give them power. Giving them that power will empower my son to make a stupid decision, one I don't think I'd be able to protect him from.

"Good. Quiet." He rubs his hands together. "I fixed the leaky faucet in the bathroom."

"How? Have you taken a plumbing class?"

"No, but it's all available on YouTube. It was kinda fun, actually. Maybe I'll be a plumber. That's a good job, right?" He sounds worried, like he's honestly concerned with how I'm going to judge him.

"Plumbing is a great job. People always need plumbers." He grins at me, and I force myself to smile back. It's wonderful to see him looking so excited about something. But I'm still nervous about how this conversation is going to go. "Hey, listen. I'm going back to work later to talk to someone."

"Who?" He perks up. "The blackmailer?"

"It doesn't matter," I begin.

But he stops me, holding his hand up. "Yes, it does. Are you going to talk to the blackmailer, Mom?"

I think about Carla at the park, how shocked I'd been to recognize her, and I nod. "Yes."

"I'm coming with you."

"Absolutely not. The last thing I want is for you two to come face-to-face. What if I've got her willing to back off and seeing you changes her mind? No, I'm going to handle this. On my own."

"What if she's dangerous?"

Carla isn't dangerous. Then again, I never thought she'd have the guts to blackmail my son while living right down the street. I think about how kind she's been at work, how well she's pretended she has no idea what's going on, and my face flames.

"You think she might be dangerous, I can tell." He looks triumphant, like he caught me in a lie. "You're worried she might try something. I'm not letting you go alone, Mom."

"Yes, but I can handle myself." *Right?*

"I'll wait in the car. I'll drive you and then wait."

"She doesn't know I'm coming," I say, then immediately realize my mistake.

Dave tilts his head to the side a little, like I'm a fascinating creature he's watching. "This isn't planned? She didn't agree to meet with you?"

I shake my head.

"What do you think is going to happen? That she'll just agree to back off?"

"Of course she will." I have to sound confident even though I do not, in any way, shape, or form, think she's willingly going to back down. She has the high road on this one, and she knows it. What I don't tell Dave, though, is that I'm willing to take things a step further if necessary.

But if I tell him that, he'll just want to leap to that course of action.

"Riiight." He draws the word out as long as possible. "She already took your earrings. Our money. She knows we can't stand up to her, and why would she even let us try? I'm coming with you. Let me help you out." He crosses his arms, leans back against the doorframe.

In an instant, his entire body language changes. Just a moment ago, he was my sweet boy, but now he's angry with me. I'm tired of seeing that dark expression on his face, especially when he's been so good other times. It's like I never really know what Dave I'm going to be getting, and it's becoming exhausting.

I just want my little boy back.

But he's not my little boy. He's angry, still glaring at me. His jaw is tight, his muscle working, like he's chewing the words he wants to say to me instead of just letting me know what he's thinking.

"You can drive me," I say, because I don't really think I have a choice in the matter. If I don't make this concession, then Dave is going to be infuriating, trying to get me to relent, doing everything he can until the moment I leave.

And what if he just won't let me leave on my own? I refuse to think about that. No, even though I don't want him there with me, inviting him and making him think he's included is the best option I have.

"Good." He nods, looking just like his father did when he finally got his way about something. It's uncanny, but I don't say anything. "I'm glad you came around, Mom. I don't want you to screw this up."

I frown. "I'm not the one who got us into this situation in the first place," I say, but whatever else I was going to say dies in my throat. The expression on Dave's face is so angry, so dark, that I wish I hadn't said anything at all.

"What, you blame me for what's happening?"

Yes, I do. Even though I wish I didn't. "Of course not. It was an accident."

"You're right. An accident. I don't want you to forget that, Mom. And here I am, trying to be helpful. Trying to be *good*, like you want me to be." He spins away from me and stalks into the house.

I step inside after him, taking in all the tools on the kitchen floor. Some of them I recognize; they're old and rusted, ones that came with the house when I bought it. Others, though, those are new. They still have stickers on them.

"Where did you get these tools?" My heart beats hard in my chest as I wait for him to answer. For a moment, I'm not sure that he's going to. He's paused by the bottom of the stairs, one hand on the railing, and he doesn't immediately turn around. "Dave, where—"

"I heard you," he snaps, then whips around to face me. "We needed them, so I got them."

"But where? And how? I had the car. I was gone all day."

"From the store." He bares his teeth at me a little bit. He looks feral when he does that, like a huge cat backed into a corner. I know there's no way I could reach out and touch him without him ripping my arm off. "I had a friend drive me."

My stomach sinks. "Jeremy?"

"Don't ask questions you don't want to know the answers to. You're welcome, by the way." He waves his arm at the mess behind me. "Geez, you'd think you could be a bit more grateful, but no. All you want to do is find things that I've done wrong. Jesus, Mom."

I can't speak as I watch him hurry up the stairs to his room. Finally, I turn, my eyes flicking across the mess on the floor. In addition to the tools, there are some wet towels, a puddle of water. Sure, he fixed this for me, and I thought at first it would be a great thing, something to celebrate, but now the excitement has soured. I can taste it in my mouth, like I've sucked on a lemon.

Even though I haven't ever bought tools myself, I know how expensive they are. I'm well aware that there are hundreds of dollars of tools sitting on my kitchen floor and that my son stole them all. I squat down, holding my head in my hands, trying to get rid of the pounding there.

I thought I could handle him. I really thought that he'd see the light, that he'd understand that he can't just treat people like crap, that he can't continually get away with doing whatever it is he wants.

But what if I'm wrong?

What if I'm not strong enough to control my son?

37

"Park there," I say, pointing to a dark part of the parking lot. "Carla doesn't know we're coming, and the last thing I want is for her to look out and see us pulling up."

I feel sick. If I hadn't told Dave my plan about coming back here to confront Carla, I don't think I would have gone through with it. I'd be much happier sitting at home, watching TV, drinking some hot water with lemon. Hell, I'd be happier running a marathon, and running's for chumps. Anything would be better than going down this path, but I don't have a choice.

Dave does as I say without argument, pulling the car to a stop under a broken light. There's no way Carla will see us out here; we're not only in the dark, we're in a blind spot from the diner. She'd have to peek out the side window of the place, crane her neck to the left, and know what she was looking for to see us.

It's the best place to hide.

"You stay here," I say, gripping my key as hard as I can.

I'm going to need it to get into the diner. "I'm going to talk to her, okay? I know I can talk some sense into her, but if you show up and are angry or acting out, then I don't think she's going to listen to us."

He nods, already brushing me off. "But if things go south, I'll step in."

"No." My voice is firm. "Things aren't going to go south, Dave, and if they do, I'm going to be the one to take care of it. I've planned it out."

He sounds surprised. "You've planned out how to kill your friend?"

That's all I did this afternoon. I couldn't eat. I couldn't read. I cleaned up Dave's mess and thought about how to end Carla if I needed to.

Poison. I see why it's always been popular with women. I don't know any other way to do it.

"I have, and I've got it under control."

But could I do it?

"I'm impressed, Mom. You have more balls than I would have given you credit for. Alright, best of luck in there." He waves his hand at the diner.

There are only a few lights on inside as Carla cleans by herself. I watch for a moment and see her walk in front of the windows. Since I've closed with her before, I know what's going on. She has music turned up loud. Coffee brewing. Her feet are tired, I'm sure they are, but she's still dancing from time to time.

She's happy.

I'm going to end it.

Swallowing hard, I get out and carefully close the car door so it doesn't slam and alert Carla to my presence. Keeping my head down, I hurry across the parking lot.

There aren't any cameras here because Richard is too cheap to install them, but I don't want anyone driving by to recognize me.

Not that I look like I normally do. I'm wearing one of Dave's big hoodies and a pair of jeans. My hair is in a ponytail, and I have a ball cap pulled down over my forehead. I did my best to make sure people wouldn't be able to easily pick me out of a crowd if they did see me.

The closer I get to the diner, the more worried I am, but I push those thoughts aside and unlock the door. Step in. Lock it behind me. Just like I thought, music blares from the stereo in the kitchen. Ace of Base, Carla's favorite.

She's not here, which means she's probably in the back, filling up the salt and pepper shakers. I take a deep breath and walk through the dining area, pushing open the swinging doors into the kitchen.

"Carla," I say, unable to stop myself, unable to make myself wait. I suddenly want this over more than anything in the world.

She screams. Jumps. When she turns around, she holds a salt shaker out at me like she can use it for a weapon. "Anne Marie, holy shit! What are you doing here?"

"I just wanted to talk." I take in the salt, and my lips twist. "I'm not a slug, so you can put down your weapon."

A nervous laugh but she does just that. "I don't think now is the best time."

To talk, or for you to put down your weapon?

"It is." My head feels light. The lights back here are so bright they're disorienting, and I give my head a little shake. "Come talk with me, Carla. We'll have some coffee. We need to clear the air."

She pauses, but I don't blame her. Would I willingly sit

and talk with me if the roles were reversed? I don't know that I would, but she doesn't have a choice. I'm not going to give her one.

"Okay." She brushes past me, and I follow her, watching as she pours us each a cup of coffee. We sit at a high-top table in the corner of the diner.

I wonder if Dave can see us, but I don't turn to look out the windows.

"Okay, talk." She pushes my cup towards me, and I take it, wrapping my hands around it to draw warmth from the coffee. "I know what you're going to say, though."

"What is that?"

"That you want me to stop." She lifts her chin and stares me right in the eyes. "But you don't know what I saw. You don't know how terrible it was. He deserves to be punished, Anne Marie. He's just as bad as the drunk driver who killed my dad."

"Then why didn't you go to the police?" My heart hammers at the thought, but I ignore the fear of him dressed in orange, his hands and feet handcuffed anytime he's taken anywhere. "Why torture him? Why steal my things?"

"Would you have rather I called the cops?" She tilts her head and stares at me like I'm an exotic bug.

"No," I admit. "But this isn't sustainable, Carla. The stealing? The blackmail?"

She frowns. Straightens up. "You told me he's been better. You've been talking about how amazing he's been, and that's because of me. You know what you should be doing, Anne Marie?" She doesn't give me time to answer. "Thanking me."

"Thanking you?"

She's right, you know. You thought it too, but now you don't want to admit it.

"Yes. For scaring him into being a good kid because obviously nothing else was working."

I can't believe her. Shock must play across my face because she laughs and calls me out on it.

"Don't look so surprised. Dave's a mess."

"I know," I say softly, and her eyebrows fly up. "I know he's a mess, and I know I should do something about it, but I don't know what to do." I debate what to say next to get her to understand, to get her on my side of this. "I'm going to get him a therapist. He's a good kid, Carla; he just made a mistake."

"He killed a man."

"And it was a mistake. Believe me, he's torn up about it. You're right, he's been better when he's scared, and that just shows me how good he can be." I'm desperate, and it must show through in my words because she doesn't interrupt me. "Just...let me handle this, okay? No more blackmail. Don't ruin the rest of his life over a stupid mistake."

Nothing.

"We've all made mistakes," I say, trying a different tactic. "But he feels remorse. He's sorry. He tells me that all the time."

"Really?" She takes a sip of her coffee, slurping it loudly. I still haven't tried mine.

"Really." *Lies.* "He's not a bad kid, Carla. He made a mistake. And he wants to move past it, but he can't when you keep holding it over his head." *And if you don't let it go, Carla, I'll kill you, I swear I will.*

Anything for my son.

She sighs. Leans back in her chair.

Ace of Base is still screaming through the stereo, and I'm starting to get a headache, but I refuse to look away from her. Everything hinges on what she does. What she decides.

"He was pretty old. Mr. George."

I nod. *Is it working?*

"And kinda mean."

I can't breathe.

"Okay, Anne Marie, listen. You get that boy of yours in therapy, okay? You get him the help he needs and make sure he doesn't step out of line again. Can you do that?"

"I can." *I will.*

"Fine." She sighs, rubbing the spot between her eyebrows. "I can't believe I'm agreeing to this. But if he steps one toe out of line again, I promise you, I'm going to come back. Or call the cops, I don't know. A drunk driver ruined my family. I don't...I don't want to do the same to yours. Just make sure he doesn't act out again. Ever."

"He won't." I think about the stolen tools on my kitchen floor. "Thank you."

"Sure, whatever." A small smile. "Help me close up. I want to get out of here."

I do that, rinsing our mugs and putting them in the sink for the dishwasher to tackle in the morning. She finishes the salt and pepper shakers, and then we walk outside. It's getting cool out, and clouds have moved in, threatening a storm later. Carla takes her time locking the door, then rattles it hard to make sure it's not going to open.

"I'll see you tomorrow," I say.

She shakes her head. "I'm off tomorrow. Perk of working a double today." Her eyes grow hard. "I'm serious about what I said, Anne Marie. One toe."

"I know. Thank you." I consider trying to hug her, but

we're not the hugging type, so I give her a half wave. "I'm parked over here," I say, jutting my thumb over my shoulder.

"I'm there." She points to her car under a lamp, the light around it like a halo, a protective circle. "Be good, Anne Marie. Don't let me regret this."

"I won't." I stand still, watching as she walks to her car. From where Dave parked, I hear the engine grumble to life. Nice that he's willing to come pick me up so I don't have to walk over there in the dark. I turn, looking for him.

No headlights.

A squeal of tires.

Carla pauses, looks up.

All of the spit in my mouth dries, and my tongue feels thick and heavy, an eel, not a muscle I can move. "Carla," I gasp out, trying to convince my muscles to run to her. My legs are on strike, but I manage a few steps. "Carla! Run!"

She turns to look at me, her mouth falling open. For a moment there's just confusion on her face; then her expression changes. Hardens.

My Camry slams into her. Her body flies, limbs askew, her hair flying out from her body. For a moment she's suspended in air, and I think that she'll be fine, she'll turn and land on her feet, even though I know it's only cats that know how to do that.

She slams to the ground. It's a sickening crunch, one of breaking bones and wet meat slapped onto the ground.

I can't move.

The window rolls down. Dave leans over so he can yell at me. "Mom, move!"

One step, then another.

I should go to her. I should check if she's breathing. I should—

"Mom! We have to go!"

I need to call 911. Or at least check on her.

Maybe move the body.

"Mom!"

I know what I should do.

But instead I get in the car.

38

"Wahoo!" The windows are down, and Dave reaches out, slapping his hand on the roof of the car. "Did you see that? Did you see how I took care of it, Mom? She won't be bothering us any longer!"

I can't move. Tears streak down my cheeks, and I squeeze my hands together as hard as possible, letting my fingernails bite into my skin. It hurts. I welcome it.

"That was amazing! Try to blackmail me and see what happens!" He whoops again, flying through a stop sign, then taking a curve so fast I feel myself leaning towards him. "Can you believe how she *flew*?"

"Dave." His name is dust and dry in my mouth. I swallow and try again. "Dave, what the hell was that?"

"That was me taking care of it." He turns to look at me. "You're welcome, by the way. I know there wasn't any way you were going to get through to her. She's crazy, Mom. She wasn't going to stop."

I turn away from him and stick my face out the window. Air buffets me, the sound painful in my ears, but at least I don't have to listen to my son right now. I don't want to close my eyes because all I see is Carla's body flying through the air, twisting, then that landing.

That's a sound I'm never going to be able to forget.

"Dave, she agreed." I turn back to him, clawing at his arm. *How could he be so stupid? So rash?*

"What?" He glances at me, then back at the road. Our headlights slice through the night like a scalpel. "What did you say?"

"Roll up the windows!" I can't hear a damn thing, not with the wind whipping around us like this. I need him to listen, and I need to hear myself think. There are a dozen voices screaming in my head right now, and I don't know which one to focus on.

"Fine, geez. I thought you'd be happy I took care of the problem." He mashes down on the buttons on the door, and the windows slowly roll up. "Happy?"

No. "Dave, she was going to stop."

"What?" He pulls up to a red light, the last one we'll be at all the way home. From here to there it's a curvy road, dark, lonely.

"Carla. She agreed to stop. No more blackmail. She wasn't going to go to the police, either. She was going to let you live your life." It's not entirely the truth, but what does it matter? It's not like Carla is going to come back and argue with me, tell me that she wasn't really going to back down, that the blackmail was always going to hang as a threat over Dave's head.

But what if she's not dead?

The thought slams into me, and I grab my chest. I should have checked. She might be alive; she might be there on the pavement, wondering what happened, choking to death on her own blood, ready to tell everyone what we did.

"She wasn't going to stop." He sounds confident and guns it when the light turns green. "She was lying to you."

"No." I shake my head, unable to get the mental image of Carla gasping for breath out of my mind. "No, she wasn't, Dave. You messed up. She was going to let you go."

He scoffs. Doesn't look at me.

"We have to go back." I announce this like I'm sure he's going to follow directions. "Dave, I'm serious. What if Carla isn't dead? We can still fix this, okay?"

He doesn't answer, but I notice the way his grip tightens on the steering wheel.

"Dave, she could still be alive. What if we can help her? Then you won't have killed her. We can say it was an accident."

"But it wasn't."

"Nobody has to know. She'll forgive you."

No, she won't.

But I ignore that thought. I'm desperate for him to listen to me, and I grab his arm. "Please, Dave. Take me back. Let me call 911 if she needs help, if she can still survive."

"Are you stupid?" He doesn't slow down. If anything, he drives faster. "What, you think the police will just forgive us if she's alive and tells them what happened?"

"I didn't do anything."

"Sure you did. You let me come. You and I talked about the fact that I would handle things with her if you couldn't." He turns to grin at me. "You gave me the green light to end her, so I did."

"No. None of that happened."

He shrugs. "Why do you think the police would believe you over me? I'm just a kid. You talked me into it."

Panic grips my throat. "No, you're the one who's always in trouble. I'm a good person, Dave! I go to work. I help people out. I don't get in trouble. I'm not selling drugs or stealing tools or skipping class."

This can't be happening.

He shrugs, the movement lazy, like he doesn't care what happens between the two of us.

I want to scream at him for how calm he's being about this, for how much he obviously doesn't seem to care. It's not fair, not fair that I've done so many things for him and he's willing to treat me like this.

"But is that something you want to risk? Are you so sure about that?"

I don't answer. It's not that I can't speak, but now I don't know what to say.

"That's what I thought. Listen, Mom, I know this isn't how you wanted the night to go, but it really is for the best. Carla wasn't going to keep our secret. She couldn't. She'd want more and more from us, and eventually we wouldn't have any more to give. You really think she'd be fine with letting us walk away from her? I don't."

Maybe he's right. Maybe Dave is right. He's always been really good at reading people and knowing their true intentions, so why should this be any different? I tend to always look for the good in people, and I know I'm a bit gullible. There's no reason why I shouldn't believe him.

He and I want the same thing.

Right?

"Okay." From the corner of my eye I see how much he relaxes at that one word. He was worried about what I was going to say, and that surprises me. "You're right, Dave. Let's just go home."

"Good." He stretches, taking both hands off the wheel for a moment. "It's the best idea, Mom. Listen, we'll get through this, okay? There really isn't anything that can stop us as long as the two of us work together. We're a team, and nothing can break us when we have each other's backs. Tonight I showed you how much I had yours."

"Just promise me one thing," I say, and I wait for him to glance at me before I continue, "I want you to be good. You were when you were scared, you realize that, right?" He nods, and I continue, "Why can't we have that all the time? Why can't you go to school and not steal and just be good?"

A long pause. We're almost to our road now and haven't seen a single other vehicle. I wonder how long Carla will lie in the parking lot before someone finds her, but I can't think about that right now. She's gone. Dave isn't.

And Dave has been the only thing that mattered to me for a long, long time.

"I'll be good. As good as I can be."

That's all I need from him. I exhale hard, finally relaxing into the seat.

He'll be good. I know he will.

But what if he's not?

Then I'll make sure he is.

39

TUESDAY

I'm nervous going to work in the morning. My clothes don't seem to fit right; my skin feels too tight; my shoes pinch. My entire body feels like it's on high alert, but there isn't anything I can do about it. I consider asking Dave what he's going to get up to today, but I don't know that I can bear the answer.

I don't want to know the truth. I want to picture him behaving, doing what he's supposed to do. The thought of what he might get up to while I'm gone is too much for me to bear.

Even though I shouldn't have been surprised by the police tape and blue lights in the parking lot, my heart beats in my throat as I pull up to the diner. There's a small group of regulars off to the side, all of them watching what's going on. Standing right in front of them is Richard, his chest puffed out, his hands hanging uselessly at his sides.

I park, not in the back, where I normally do, because there are too many lookie-loos. I'm off to the side of the diner. Check my reflection. Then I get out and hurry to Richard.

I've never been in a play. Never once in my life did I think that standing up on a stage in front of a group of strangers and acting sounded like fun, but that's exactly what I have to do right now. I need to pretend I don't know anything about what's going on, and I have to sell it.

"Richard," I gasp out, pushing through the group of people to get to my boss. "What in the world's going on? Is everything okay?"

He turns to me, anger etched into the lines around the eyes, evident in the way he's holding his mouth. "I got to work this morning to do the books, and I found her in the parking lot."

"Who?" *Just pretend like you don't know anything. That's the only way through this.*

He points, and I turn, following the line of his finger. From here I can only see some EMTs. They're bent over something on the ground. There's a loud zipping sound, and they move back.

A body bag.

"Who's in the bag?" I don't have to try to put a note of panic in my voice. It's there whether I want it or not.

"Carla."

"What? No." I exhale hard, unable to help myself. For a moment I'd almost convinced myself that she was alive, that she'd survived Dave plowing into her, that she would have picked herself up off the pavement after we left and gone home. Or to the police. The hospital.

But we would have heard about it, right? If she'd gone to the police, they would have been knocking on our door last night. And if she'd gone to the hospital, then it would have been all over the news. People eat that sort of thing up, don't they? I remember all too well how George's death was on the news over and over until it wasn't.

"I found her." Richard isn't speaking to me, he's just speaking. His eyes have a faraway look in them that makes me nervous. "I came in, and she was there, just there, and I thought maybe she fell, so I went to help her." He closes his eyes, and when he opens them, he turns to look at me. "There was so much blood."

I feel my stomach twist. The contents are trying to come up, but I swallow hard. Keep them down. "Do they know what happened?" I'm well aware of the police standing by the EMTs, how the one closest to us keeps looking over his shoulder at the crowd. "Was she sick? A heart attack?"

I'm trying to plant seeds that I don't have any clue about what really happened to Carla. When Richard is questioned again, if my name comes up, I want him to think back on how confused I was and tell the police officer that I couldn't possibly have been involved.

"She was hit by a car. Her arms were all..." His voice trails off, and he twists his arms out at painful angles from his body. "And the side of her face...she was missing some of her face."

I'm going to throw up. I close my eyes and count to ten, taking deep breaths to stop myself from getting sick. When I open them again, an officer is staring at me.

I wouldn't really pay attention to it, but I noticed him right when I walked up. He looked familiar. He looked...

It's the same officer who came by my house when Dave killed George. Waddell.

"I'm going to go open the diner," I say, ducking my head

so the officer can't see me straight on. "We need to open, or our customers are going to go somewhere else."

"What? Oh, right." He sounds distracted, and I take him by the arm, pulling him with me. "Trust me, Richard, you'll feel better with some coffee." I lower my voice. "Do you have whiskey?"

He nods.

Good. I'll make him something to drink and put him in his office, where the shock can wear off. As much as I'd love a shot of whiskey as well, I can abstain. I'll wait until I get home.

Home. I'm moving faster now as I unlock the front door of the diner and push Richard through it. "Give me five minutes to start the coffee," I call out to the crowd. "You go to your office, okay? Have a drink if that's what you need. I'll take care of things out here."

"Thank you." He scrubs his hand down his face and sighs. "Seriously, Anne Marie, I don't know what I'd do without you right now. But you're right, we need to open. We need to move on like nothing happened."

"I think that's the best thing to do right now. You go back to your office, and I'll bring you some coffee in a few minutes. It'll be fine, Richard. I've got this."

"So glad I didn't fire you," he mumbles, then turns and stumbles across the dining area.

I wait until he's in the kitchen before I follow and start the coffee; then I pull my phone from my pocket. My hands shake as I tap the icon to find where Dave is. He has to be at school. He has to be where he belongs.

But he's not. The little blue dot blinks at me from a location I don't recognize. "Dammit," I mutter, closing the app and tapping the phone icon to call him.

The front door opens. The jangle of the bell makes me lean out through the kitchen's double doors. "Just a few more minutes," I call, but I don't take my eyes from my phone.

I'm about to tap the green call button when heavy foot-steps make me pause. Look up.

My stomach sinks.

It's the police officer.

40

The officer raises his hand in greeting, then looks around the diner slowly, soaking in every detail.

I freeze, my mind racing. Carefully, because I'm afraid to make any sudden movements right now, I slip my phone back into my pocket.

"Ms. Kerns?" The officer blinks at me like he's trying to remember if he knows me.

I find myself nodding even though the only thing I want to do right now is flee. "Hi, yes. Can I help you? We're not open yet, but I'm more than happy to bring you a cup of coffee outside in just a few minutes." How do I sound? Normal? Terrified?

"I don't want coffee. I was hoping to talk to you for a minute."

Of course you were.

"Sure, I have just a minute. I do need to get started for the day, though. Don't want to get in trouble with my boss." I throw a glance over my shoulder toward Richard. Of course, the one time I need the man hovering around me, he's not here. Figures. Sighing, I turn back to the officer, then walk closer to him.

That's what a totally innocent person would do, right? They'd walk over to him, talk to him, not act like they know something terrible. Still, I feel like my joints are all uncomfortable, like each step is new, like my body is going to betray me.

The sound of the back door opening makes me whip around. *Richard?* But it's not. Our cook leans through the door, sees me with the officer, salutes me, then disappears again.

"You worked with the deceased?" He watches me as I pull out a chair and sit, but doesn't join me at the table.

Immediately I regret sitting down. There's something about being lower than another person that makes it feel like they're in complete control.

"Carla?" He nods, and I swallow hard. "Yes, I've worked with Carla for years."

"And you live on the same street as her?"

"I do." I spread my hands on my lap, then grip my thighs, squeezing as hard as I can. I want to distract myself from what's happening, what's being said.

"Did you ever notice anyone following her? Watching her?"

"Following her?" I frown, doing my best to look like I'm really thinking through his question. "No, but you've been on our street, Officer. It's not like I could see her house from mine. Someone could have been following her, I guess, but I wouldn't have ever known about it."

"Fair enough. Do you think she had any ties to your other neighbor George Reece?"

"Not that I know of." I have to bite my lip to keep from

asking questions. Having watched more than my fair share of *SVU* when Dave was younger and just wouldn't sleep at night, I know better than to offer up any information that the officer could later use against me. Sure, he seems nice, but that's just what he wants me to think.

"That case is still open." He stretches, looking down at me like he's trying to read my mind. "It's just a strange coincidence that two of your neighbors have been run over by a car, don't you think?"

"Is that how she died?" I gasp, covering my mouth. "Oh my God, that's terrible. I thought maybe she had a heart attack or something else. But to get hit by a car?"

He frowns. "Is that your Camry out there?"

I don't have to look to know that he's jutting his thumb right at my car. I do glance in that direction, however, and my heart sinks when I see two officers walking around it.

"It is. Why?"

"Just asking." A long pause. "What happened to your window?"

"Someone broke it out," I say, refusing to throw Dave under the bus. "I was going to file a police report but was so busy with work that I lost track of the time. Then I didn't have any proof of who it might be, so I let it go. I'm going to get it fixed as soon as I make enough in tips to cover the repairs."

He doesn't respond. The silence stretches out between us until I hear the sound of the coffeepot finishing its cycle. "I'll let you get to work. But if you think of anything, any connection between the two of them, give me a call."

"I will," I say, hoping I sound earnest. "Thank you for taking this so seriously." Tears well up in my eyes, and I don't know if they're because I'm scared or because of how awful it really was to see Carla get hit right in front of me last night. I keep remembering how she was thrown through the air, the sick sound her body made when she landed.

I give my head a little shake to clear the thoughts.

"Have a good day. Call me. If you know something, you need to tell me. It's the only way we can get justice for George and Carla. You want that, don't you?" His gaze bores into me, and I nod.

"Of course I do," I say. I stand completely still, watching as he lets himself out of the diner. He stalks across the parking lot, hardly looking at the crowd, which keeps growing. My heart drops as he walks right over to my Camry.

The officer there shrugs. Points at the dents on the back bumper, the side door. He gestures to the broken window; then the two of them turn and walk away from my car.

I exhale hard, bending over to combat the wave of dizziness that washes over me.

When I straighten back up, I have a smile on my face. I walk to the front door and open it, lean out, and call: "Breakfast! Come on in, but be patient. It's going to be a long morning."

My regulars pat me on the shoulder as they walk past me. Some of them murmur words of consolation, but others stare out into the parking lot after they're seated, watching the spot where Carla died like they're going to be able to see what I saw last night.

I stare out the window with them, my mind replaying over and over what happened. I see her bounce off the car's bumper. I see how she twisted and turned, taking flight, which isn't something that any human should ever do.

But then I try to look away from her. It's hard, because I was staring at her while everything happened, but I wanted to see Dave. I wanted to know what he looked like while he pressed down hard on the gas, his hands tight on the steering wheel, his focus on Carla and Carla alone.

Did he even see me standing there watching her leave?

Was he so intent on her and what was about to happen that he couldn't look away?

Was he frowning? Upset? Did he know that what he was doing was wrong?

Or was he happy about it? Excited, even?

"Anne Marie, are you okay?" A customer reaches out and lightly touches my arm.

I jerk back, a gasp escaping my lips. "I'm sorry," I say, "I was just...it's just. Carla. I can't believe what happened."

I can't believe my son killed her.

"It's fine, Anne Marie; take your time. We're not in a rush, and I know this morning is going to be hard for you." The woman smiles at me, but the rest of her table is looking out the window. "It's such a tragedy. How anyone could hurt sweet Carla is beyond me. I don't think she ever did anything wrong in her life."

"Me either," I say. "She was such a good person. Now, what can I get started for you?"

The diner is filling up around me. Some of the people I know from coming by every morning for coffee and a muffin, but some are new. Are they here just because of what happened last night? I know people love to gossip, that bad news spreads faster than good, but is it possible they're all just here to rubberneck?

"Coffee would be great," the woman says.

"Coffee, right. I'll be right back with that." I'm antsy to get into the back. To check my phone.

To figure out exactly where my son is.

41

Five messages.

That's how many I left for Dave, each one more and more worried as he refused to pick up. I have no idea where my son is, no idea what he might be doing, but for the first time, I really know what he's capable of.

And that's what terrifies me.

Slowing down, I turn onto our gravel road and straighten out the car, pushing the gas down as far as I'm willing to. Carla's house is right here, the driveway packed with cars, but I don't look away from the road.

I don't want to see anyone there. More than that, though, I don't want anyone to see me watching, to wonder what I might know, to read my face and tell that I know the truth.

As much as I want to speed away, I know what will happen if I go too fast. It's the same thing I warned Dave about time and time again when he got his provisional license. It's too easy to fishtail, to slip on the gravel, to accidentally slam the car into a tree.

I can't imagine my sweet boy dying like that.

"But where were you all day, Dave?" My mouth is dry, and I lick my lips, feeling the crack forming there on my bottom lip. All day I've been on my feet, trying to keep a smile on my face, dealing with customers who want more than just coffee and pancakes.

They all wanted information. They wanted to know what happened to Carla, wanted me to willingly spill the beans, but I couldn't. All I could say was that she was hit, it was an accident, and nobody knows who did it.

But only one of those things is the truth.

There's a for sale sign by George's driveway, and my stomach clenches as I drive past it.

Finally, I reach my driveway, and I pull in, exhaling hard in relief when I see there isn't another car in the driveway. All day I've had the terrible feeling that Dave was out with Jeremy, that I was going to have to deal with him bringing home more drugs, or going out selling them, or something. The last thing we need right now is any police interest.

We need to lie low.

I park the car and stare at the house, wondering what I'm going to walk into. There's a part of me terrified of going inside. This part wants to sit in the car and let the rest of the day pass me by. Hell, why stop there? Why not let the week pass, the month, maybe even the year?

Let the seasons change, let the fallen leaves cover the car before snow comes like a thick blanket, closing me in my Camry, unable to get out, unable to deal with what else Dave might have done.

But I can't do that. Someone has to protect my son. If not from other people, because he's proven that he can handle that himself, then from himself. Dave will self-destruct if I'm not there to stop him. To keep him on the high road. To ensure he doesn't fly too close to the sun.

"Oh, Icarus," I say, getting out, then shake my head. "I'm not going to let my Dave turn out just like you." Confidence makes me straighten my back as I walk up to the porch. I have a goal now, to protect my son, the same goal I've had for sixteen years.

I lost sight of it for a while, but I'm back.

Dave is my little boy, and I'm always going to take care of him, no matter what. I never liked that creepy kids' book with the mom who climbed through her son's window to rock him to sleep, but I feel like I get it now. I understand how crazy she felt about her son, how willing she was to do whatever it took to protect him. He might not get it, might not want me there for him like I am, but he can't stop me from looking out for him.

Now I just want to see him, and I hurry to the front door and let myself in. "Dave, I'm home!"

There's loud music coming from his bedroom, and I feel myself relax. All is right with my world. This morning was hard, and work will continue to be hard until Richard hires someone to replace Carla, but I'll get through it. I've gotten through worse.

And as long as I know Dave is safe, I'm okay. Dropping my purse, I wander into the kitchen to pour myself a glass of wine. It's early to be drinking, but I feel like celebrating. The cops don't know what happened. Even though I was convinced last night that we should go back for Carla's body, everything is fine.

It's the second time in my life I've been grateful my Camry is a dented-up junker.

A giggle escapes my lips, and I drown it with a sip of

wine before walking to the sink to put the empty bottle inside so I can rinse it. I recycle. I'm a good citizen.

But what I see there makes me pause. I know the knife. It's from our knife block.

But what I don't know is why it's covered in blood.

42

"Dave?" Terror makes my voice high and tight as I call Dave. I race up the stairs, barely noticing how loud the music is. The closer I get to his room, the more deafening the beat, but I don't care about that. I only care about seeing my son.

"Dave!" I pound on his door, then finally throw it open, scanning the room, desperate to see him.

There. On the bed. He's curled up on his side, his back to me, and I have a sudden, intrusive thought that the blood on the knife is his. That someone knows what he did and came here to punish him. That I'm too late.

It's not a skinned knee, not something I can fix with a kiss and a Band-Aid. If he's been stabbed—

He rolls over. His arm swings out from the bed, and he whacks his stereo, hitting the power button, the sudden quiet hurting my ears.

"Dave, are you okay?" I hurry to him and kneel by his bed. I don't see any blood, but what if he got stabbed in the stomach? That would explain why he was curled up like that. He was protecting himself, or trying to, and now I have to find the wound, have to make a decision about what to do so I can save him.

"I'm fine." He frowns, his brow furrowing, and sits up. "What? What's wrong? Why are you shrieking at me?"

"I saw the knife," I say, relief making me sag against the side of his bed. "I thought you were hurt."

He laughs. "Why would I be hurt?"

Now I'm confused. I close my eyes, picturing the knife in the sink. It did have blood on it, didn't it? "Because the knife was bloody, and you weren't answering me. I thought—"

"You thought someone snuck in here, stabbed me, left the knife in the kitchen sink for you to find, and then escaped?"

"I didn't know." I lift my chin.

"That's stupid. There would be fingerprints on it." He stares at me, then rolls his eyes. "No, I left it there for you to wash."

"What?"

"I left it there for you to get the blood off it." He speaks slowly like he thinks I can't understand what he's saying. But I do. I just don't want to.

"Whose blood is it, Dave?" I stand, adrenaline coursing through my body. It makes it difficult for me to focus on my son, this desire to run. It makes it difficult, but I'm not going to leave him here, not when I know he needs me.

He pauses, smiles.

"Dave, tell me." I'm desperate, and I'm sure he can hear it in my voice. He has to, judging by the way he smiles at me before he answers.

"Jeremy's."

"What?" I exhale hard, trying to wrap my mind around

what he just said. "What do you mean, *Jeremy's*? Did you do something to him?"

"I took care of him." He stares at me, frowning. "I thought that was what you wanted. He was trouble; you said so yourself. He broke in here. I didn't want him to be an issue in the future."

I turn, and my legs give out, causing me to sink onto the bed next to my son. Instead of putting his arm around me, which is what I really want, he shifts away from me.

"You killed Jeremy?" My voice sounds far away to me. I turn to make sure someone else isn't in the room speaking. I can't believe those words are coming out of my mouth.

"Sure. It was the smart move."

"The smart move." I can't wrap my mind around that. No matter which way I look at it, I don't see how this was the smart move.

I swallow hard and make myself look at him. For the first time in sixteen years, I can't see him as my little boy. I blink, hard, keeping my eyes closed for longer than necessary, then look at him again.

There he is. There's my little boy. In his hand is...something. He's so little, and his little hand is squeezed tightly around something small, something green.

I see stems.

No, not stems. *Legs.*

Legs hang down from his hand. The frog doesn't move.

No. I'm back in Dave's bedroom, his blue bedspread soft between my fingers. I don't even realize I've been twisting it, trying to work out some of the stress I feel, until Dave puts his hand over mine to stop me.

"Can you fix this, Mom?" There's hope in his voice, hope that I'm going to handle this for him.

I nod. "I can fix this," I tell him. "Yes, I can fix this, Dave. Why don't you come down for dinner in an hour or so, and I'll have it all taken care of."

"Thanks. I knew you could handle it for me." He rolls back over, grabs his phone.

I stand and turn to look at him. Anger battles fear, but I push both of those emotions away.

"Did anyone see you?" I have to know. Before I wash that knife, before I watch the blood swirl around the drain, I have to know. *Bleach, I'll need bleach so they can't find any proof of the blood.* It's insane, because it's not going to change what I do, it's not going to change the fact that I'll do anything in my power to protect him. But I ask anyway.

He responds with a heavy sigh. A moment later, he rolls over and looks at me. "No, Mom. Nobody saw. What, do you think I'm stupid?"

"You've killed three people, Dave." I don't realize what I'm saying, and then the words are out there between the two of us. "You have to stop."

This gets his attention. He props himself up on an elbow and stares at me. "Is that a threat, Mom?"

I shake my head. "No. Not at all. But, Dave, you're better than this. I raised you better." *You were better when you were so scared.* But I don't say that.

"I'm just taking care of things, Mom. You've always wanted me to be strong, to stand on my own two feet. You've always raised me not to take crap from anyone, and I'm not. What's the problem?"

"No problem. I'll handle the knife."

He flashes me a smile, the first since I've come up to his room.

Remember how he had floppy hair that hung down in

his eyes? Remember how he'd snuggle into me when we watched a movie on the sofa?

It's the same boy.

He's my son.

"I'll protect you," I say, and I finally leave his room. My mind races.

I'll protect him.

It's all I've ever done, and I'm not going to stop now.

EPILOGUE

TWO WEEKS LATER

It's a rare morning off, and I'm in the backyard, reading a book. I have to go into the diner in a few hours to work with our new waitress Richard hired. He told me yesterday that he was shocked how many people applied for the job just because they wanted to work at the same place where a person died.

I hadn't known what to say to that then, and I still don't.

There's an angry crow screaming at me from the back woods, but I ignore it. It probably wants the crackers left behind on my snack plate, but let it scream. I'm so tired of taking care of everything. It's a fine balance, and things with Dave haven't been great since he killed Jeremy.

The police reported it as a drug deal gone bad. I guess Jeremy was a worse person than I ever knew, and it doesn't seem like the cops are super interested in putting a lot of man-hours into finding his killer.

But that doesn't mean Dave has been good. Far from it, actually.

He's acting out more and more. He's out of control, skipping school, refusing to help out around the house. It's like none of the blackmail ever happened, like he didn't learn a thing.

The door behind me slams open, and I close my eyes. My peace, the little bit of peace I've found in the past two weeks since Jeremy died, is gone. I can feel Dave behind me, feel the anger wafting off him.

"What are you doing?" He sounds stressed, more than usual.

"I was napping out here," I admit. "And reading. I thought I'd get this book finished before my shift tonight, but it's just so comfortable in the sun that I passed out."

"You didn't hear anyone come by?" There's a note of panic in his voice, and I finally turn to look at him.

His eyes are wide. Bright spots of color splotch on his cheeks and neck. As I watch, he turns and looks behind him, then past me, scanning the woods like he's sure someone is there.

"No, I was sleeping. Like I said. Why? What's the problem?"

He hurries to me and drops into the chair next to me. When he leans closer to me, I smell it.

Fear.

It's a thick stench, and I wrinkle my nose, but before I can pull away from him, he presses a piece of paper into my hand. The paper itself is blue, the writing in a thick marker, like a Sharpie. "What is this?"

"Read it. I just found it on the front porch. You're sure you didn't hear anyone?"

"Dave," I begin, but he waves his hand to cut me off.

"Right. Sleeping. Just read it."

"'I know what you did,'" I say, then clear my throat. Sit up a bit higher in my chair. "'I know about all three of them.'"

A chill races down my spine.

"'I'm watching you.'" Dave points to the bottom of the paper. "You missed that part. Where they say they're watching me."

I sit very still. The crow is still screaming its fool head off, but I don't look up for it. At this point, who cares if it gets the crackers? Who cares what happens? Everything in my life right now has slowed down, almost to a stop.

"Where did you find this?" I croak out the words.

"Front porch." He taps the paper. "Who do you think left it? Is this a joke? Why would someone do this?" He sounds strangled and swallows a few times, like there's something in his throat he can't get rid of.

"I don't think it's a joke," I say, turning the paper over in my hands. "But who? Did you tell anyone what you did?"

"What? No. Why the hell would I do that? That's stupid." He gnaws on his thumbnail, and I have to resist the urge to reach out and stop him. "Jeremy probably had cameras."

I blink. This isn't how I thought the conversation was going. "Cameras?"

He nods. "Drug dealers usually do. He had cameras, and someone saw me. As for Carla, I bet she told someone about George. Insurance. That has to be it."

"Then when Carla showed up dead—" I say, following his train of thought.

"They knew it was me. Oh my God." He drops his head into his hands and groans. "But I have no idea who it is. Maybe that officer? He could know more than he's letting on."

"Maybe." I stand, unable to keep sitting. I'm nervous, and

when I'm upset like this, I need to move. It's hard to see Dave so worried, hard to sit here while he struggles through what's happening. "What are you going to do?"

He looks up at me, his face pained. He's so upset that I want to bend down and scoop him into my arms. I want to stop this pain for him, but I can't. There's nothing I can do right now, and he hates it when I hug him.

"I don't know. I don't know how to find out who it is. And they didn't say what they want."

"Maybe they're waiting for you to screw up," I offer. "If they know it's you, if they know what you've done, then it's likely they know we don't have much for them to take."

"Maybe. Yeah, that makes sense." He nods, then stands and pockets the note. "I don't know what to do." He pauses, shakes his head. "I'm going to the kitchen. I'm starving."

"Stress will do that to you," I say, then lightly touch his arm to get his attention. "Hey, Dave, I know you don't want to hear this from me right now, but you need to lie low. Follow the rules. Stop drawing attention to yourself. If the new blackmailer is just waiting for you to mess up, then don't. Keep them at bay."

He exhales and runs a hand through his hair. "You're right. That makes sense. If the other shoe is going to drop when I screw up, then I just won't screw up. I'll be on my best behavior."

"I think that's the best idea," I tell him, then watch as he walks inside. He'll be in the kitchen for a while, looking for something to eat. I know Dave. When he's stressed, he feels like he's starving, but he doesn't always find something to eat without digging around for a long time in the refrigerator.

Which means I have plenty of time on my own.

Leaving my book outside, I hurry inside, then upstairs to

my bedroom. I listen at the door for a moment to make sure Dave didn't follow me. It's not likely that he would have, but if he wanted me to make him something to eat, then I wouldn't be surprised.

But he's still downstairs. The sounds of him rummaging in the fridge reach my ears. It's frustrating that he might go ahead and eat the leftovers I have set aside for dinner, but I'm not interested in going down there and getting into an argument with him.

I close the door. Lock it. Then I walk to my bed and get on my knees, lifting my mattress and reaching under to pull out a manila folder and marker. I wait to open the folder until I'm sitting on the edge of the bed, the folder balanced on my knees.

I just need to see.

It's too early for another note, but now that it's real, now that I've put my plan in motion, I need to see the paper and marker, make sure they're still there, make sure Dave won't find them.

I flip open the folder and run my fingers along the edges of the blue paper. It's all here, a stack of it, paper I dug out of the dumpster behind the stationery store downtown. It was thrown away because someone cut the plastic wrapper and stole a few sheets, but that's fine with me.

I just needed something Dave had never seen before.

It's strange to take control of my life like this, but he pushed me. Dave pushed and pushed until I didn't have an option any longer. He only behaves when he's scared.

And he's only scared when he's being blackmailed.

I flip the folder shut and put it with the marker back under my mattress. It's heavy, my mattress, ancient and full of springs. A fine layer of sweat breaks out on my upper lip as I struggle to place it back under the mattress.

But it's there for when I need it. I'll protect my son, my little boy.

I'll do whatever it takes to keep him good, to enjoy the son I know he should be.

THANK YOU FOR READING

Did you enjoy reading *The Waitress*? Please consider leaving a review on Amazon. Your review will help other readers to discover the novel.

ABOUT THE AUTHOR

Emily Shiner always dreamed of becoming an author but first served her time as a banker and a teacher. After a lifetime of devouring stacks of thrillers, she decided to try her hand at writing them herself. Now she gets to live out her dream of writing novels and sharing her stories with people around the world. She lives in the Appalachian Mountains and loves hiking with her husband, daughter, and their two dogs.

ALSO BY EMILY SHINER

The Secret Wife

The Promise

The Caretaker

Her Perfect Life

The Stolen Child

I'm Following You

You Can't Hide

Her Husband's Secret

The Better Mother

The Waitress